WALL OF WORDS

WALL OF WORDS

Tim Kennemore

faber and faber

First published in 1982
by Faber and Faber Limited
3 Queen Square London WC1N 3AU
Filmset by Granada Graphics, Redhill, Surrey
Printed in Great Britain by
Redwood Burn Ltd, Trowbridge, Wiltshire

© *Tim Kennemore, 1982*

British Library Cataloguing in Publication Data

Kennemore, Tim
  Wall of words
  I. *Title*
  823'. 914   [J]   PZ7

ISBN 0-571-11856-9

To Antonia Forest,
with many thanks

1

IT WAS THE HOTTEST July afternoon for three years; the school holidays had just begun, and Anna was on the front lawn, busy being beautiful. More precisely, she was being a golden sun-kissed summer princess. Everything must be exactly right. *Two* straws, not one, in her glass of iced lemonade; her prettiest pink sun-dress; the folding sun-bed (the only way to stretch out in golden, sun-kissed glory) and a floppy straw hat which, unfortunately, hid rather a lot of her (golden, sun-kissed) hair. But one couldn't have everything; on the whole Anna was well pleased with the effect. She felt like an advertisement for summer holidays. One look at her, she felt, and people would be tempted to blow their hard-earned savings on two luxurious weeks in the Tates' front garden.

But all was not well. One vital ingredient was missing — the audience. There is little point in radiating loveliness when nobody is there to appreciate it, and on this particular afternoon Chisholm Avenue was infuriatingly deserted. There was not a soul in sight, except for fat pink Mr. Jenkins three doors down, and he had been in a sweaty stupor for the past two hours, collapsed in a sagging, strained-looking deck chair. Anna began to be bored. Insects buzzed; the road shimmered; Anna's legs stuck together.

9

to expensive private schools, but it had taken them in different ways. The Tates would not be going away on holiday. They could never afford it. Kim didn't mind. She was just relieved at having six weeks without school. Not that she didn't like school — she did, very much, and the past year, her second at Thornton Park Comprehensive, had been particularly good. She'd had a small speaking part in the school play; she'd played Goal Attack for the Under-Fourteen Netball Team; and she'd rounded the year off in splendid fashion by winning the long jump, and coming second in both the high jump and the two hundred metres on Junior Sports Day. That had been the best of all, and next year she would win all three or die in the attempt. But, none the less, the beginning of the holiday always came as a relief to Kim, and to all the Tates, because of Kerry. Getting Kerry to school — or trying to — cast a black shadow over every schoolday morning. Now that was over — until September, at any rate, and it might all be sorted out by September. Kim was an incurable optimist.

"Will we be able to do any cycling?" David was asking. "I wanted to ride over to Warren Hill. I went there at half term; you'd like it. But I suppose you'll have to stay here to keep an eye on the others."

"Not every day. They'll be at Gran's a lot of the time." Not that they took much looking after, anyhow: Frances was eleven, and practically lived at her friend Janice's house; Anna, despite her faults, which were horrible, was sensible for seven; and Kerry — Kerry seemed able to take pretty good care of herself. And their mother was home all day at week-ends, of course, and she had a fortnight's holiday coming up.

"I'll be free tomorrow, actually. Anna and Kerry are — er — they're — Dad's taking them out for the day." She gabbled this as quickly as she could; it was always awkward. The only really bitter quarrel she and David had ever had in a

11

lifetime's friendship had been over Kim's father. It had taken place on the Tates' roof. Kim had been talking, with great pride, of the novel — the extraordinary, unique novel — he was writing. She got quite carried away — it was so gorgeous to have a father talented enough, original enough, to do such a thing. She felt almost sorry for David, whose father was Something in the City. Worthy, yes, but dull. David, though, hadn't been impressed at all; he said that most people who wrote novels managed to do so without going off and leaving their families, didn't they? — and it wasn't fair on Kim's mother, and he thought it was an *awful* thing to do. Kim had given him a tremendous black eye; she nearly threw him off the roof. That had been eighteen months ago; it had taken six of the eighteen months before they properly got over the quarrel. And perhaps they never would, altogether — for Kim could not now talk comfortably to David about her father, and tried never to mention him at all; David, who had always thought that Kim would accept his frank opinion about anything, now knew better. Also, David now kept to his own roof.

These roofs had been their particular territory for seven years now. Kim it had been who started it, shortly after Anna's birth. Frances and Kerry had been quiet, placid babies; Anna was a screamer, with cast-iron lungs. Night and day her wails filled the house. Kim, aged six, decided to move out and live on the garage roof. It was a fair height, but Kim had long legs, a very determined nature and the wall dividing the Tate and Holder front gardens to help her on her way. She made it. Her parents were alarmed. It was too dangerous; Kim would certainly break her neck. But Kim continued to scramble up there whenever their backs were turned, and suffered nothing worse than scraped knees; Mrs. Tate decided that since she was clearly dead set on breaking her neck, it was more convenient that she should do it at home than in the park, falling from a tree, or, worse, from the top of the monster metallic slide. Kim had won; the roof was hers.

David too had a sister problem. His problem was at that time ten years old, and bossy. She ordered him about a great deal, and when David ignored the orders, which was often, she went and told their mother. The roof seemed an excellent idea to him. But it was considerably more difficult on the Holder side — a path separated garage from wall. Also, his legs were not so long as Kim's. David, however, was not a boy to give up easily, and the need to escape a nagging female can drive a man to great lengths, as Anne Boleyn discovered when her once loving husband Henry cut off her head. While Kim shouted encouragement, David manoeuvred the dustbin into position, climbed on to it, and somehow, with a little help from a friendly drainpipe, he managed to heave himself over the edge. Kim cheered; the two children beamed at each other in mutual (and in David's case, breathless) triumph. They had used the roofs ever since. When they were aged ten and eleven respectively, they nailed up a series of signs warning of the dreadful fates that awaited trespassers: Trespassers will be Exploded; Trespassers will be peeled, Chipped and Deep-Fried; Nailed to the Wall; Fed to the Wolves (Bit by Bit) . . . Nobody trespassed. Even Anna kept off Kim's roof.

Kim glanced at her watch; it was already twenty to five. "I'd better get down, I suppose," she said, reluctantly. It was so pleasantly cool up there, shielded from the sun. But Frances would be home at any moment. "I don't know about tomorrow. It's terribly hot for cycling, don't you think?"

"Let's make it the first cool day, then." Kim agreed to that, and dropped expertly into her back garden, where she found Kerry crouching on the grass, deep in silent communication with her pet tortoise, who was sitting in a glass casserole dish. Tortoise casserole for dinner? Kim moved closer, and saw that there was a very shallow layer of water in the bottom of the casserole. Ah — *poached* tortoise . . . "Speedy's having a nice cool bath," Kerry said. "It's so hot."

"*Ah*. I *see*." Tortoise slow-baked in its own shell — serve with iced turtle soup . . ."Enjoying that, are you, Speedy? Having a good splash? Going to sprint around a bit afterwards to dry off?" Speedy looked at her with wrinkled disdain. "Are you sure it's the right thing to do, Kerry? Bathing a tortoise?" Kim wasn't much worried; Kerry never went far wrong with animals.

"Oh yes, I think it's a very good idea. Well, I always give him one when he wakes in the spring, all gunged up. I'm sure he's enjoying it."

"Enjoying it? He's thrilled out of his tiny mind. Look how he's leaping about." Kim tapped the tortoise, as if to calm him down. "I've never seen him so excited." Speedy blinked and retired inside his shell. "Rejected," Kim said sadly. "Rejected by a tortoise. I'm a failure." Kerry chuckled, and stroked the shell with affection. It was just like Kerry, Kim thought — on a day like this, when all sensible people were trying busily to keep them*selves* cool, here was her daft sister bothering about a tortoise. She was a funny little scrap, Kerry — pale and thin, coppery hair cut even shorter than Kim's, a dusting of freckles on skin that had a papery-thin, almost transparent look to it. Kim liked her better than anybody in the world.

"There's Frances." A figure could be seen, moving in the kitchen. Kim tweaked her sister's ear. "Let's go in and have some lemonade."

"Anna had the last of it," Kerry said, "but it was flat anyway. I must just get Speedy out."

"Don't overdo it, buster," Kim said to the tortoise. "Strenuous exercise can strain the heart. All right. Just one quick somersault before I go." Speedy poked his head out, perhaps considering the somersault, but decided against it. "He's out of fuel." Kim tapped him again. "He runs on Shell." Kerry giggled — she liked this joke, every time she heard it.

Frances was busy getting the tea. "Cheese on toast," she said, before Kim could ask. Frances was already quite an accomplished cook, whereas Kim's efforts in the kitchen, however well-meaning and enthusiastic, had never been appreciated by her family. Given the freedom of the kitchen, plenty of recipe books and scope for trial and error — particularly error — Kim was sure she could produce the most fascinating dishes. But the Tates had tasted her cooking, and they didn't want to know. They had no *faith*. Why should they, anyway, with Mrs. Tate a highly competent, if uninterested, cook, and Frances so talented in that direction?

Cheese on toast, though — Kim sniffed. Any fool could bung a few slices of bread and cheese under the grill. Admittedly she had been *known* to burn toast, but it was perfectly easy to chop off the black bits around the edge. They wouldn't let her *try*.

Frances, humming contentedly, was slicing bread. "You might lay the table," she said, hopefully.

"I *might*," Kim said. "But it isn't likely." Their eyes met; they grinned. Kim and Frances were wildly different in appearance, character and interests, but they got along very well on the whole, complementing one another rather than clashing. Since they shared a bedroom, as well as a good deal of responsibility, this was just as well.

Anna trailed in, bearing the remains of the flat lemonade.

"You might lay the table," Kim said, knowing better.

"Frances, you said I could choose the pudding today. *And* I'm going to make it."

"*You're* making the pudding, are you?" Kim, perched on a

stool, swung her legs to and fro. Anna watched them suspiciously.

"Frances said."

"Good. We'll have Baked Alaska, then. That's a sort of cooked ice cream and meringue. Shouldn't take you five minutes."

Anna frowned — cooked *ice cream*? — and decided to ignore her. "*This* is what I'm choosing for us to have," she said, stretching up and pulling a packet from the cupboard. Kim shuddered.

"Pink creosote."

"Strawberry *Cremilite*," Anna said reprovingly, and began to read the packet. Anna read very well, and never missed an opportunity to prove it; almost, Kim thought, as if to emphasize the fact that Kerry, who was a full year older, had missed so much school that she could hardly read at all. " 'Just add a pint of milk for a delicious, creamy light dessert,' " read Anna. " 'With new Strawberry Cremilite you can enjoy the flavour of real strawberries and cream *all year round*.' " Kerry slipped through the back door and stood, listening.

"Revolting slimy pink goo," said Kim. "I don't want any. I'll have some fresh fruit. The real thing."

"Serves four," said Anna. "Good. If you don't have any that'll be just right. Oh, Kerry, you'd better lay the table. Now, let's see." She looked again at the picture on the packet: two dainty, immaculate, individual glass dishes of Cremilite, smoothly whipped with a little point in the centre. Cremilite meant a great deal to Anna. It was advertised on television by a group of children called the Cremikids. The Cremikids had the most fascinating adventures, all in the space of thirty seconds, and each adventure was rounded off with a delicious helping of Cremilite, Orange, Strawberry, Chocolate or Banana, and the singing of the Cremilite song. Anna would have given

16

five years of her life to be a Cremikid.

Kim watched as Anna emptied the pink powder carefully into a mixing bowl, took a pint of milk from the fridge and poured it on to the powder, selected a fork and began to beat. All without spilling a drop. Anna never spilt things. Kerry slipped and tripped, fumbled and bumbled, tumbled and stumbled, dropped things, broke things, knocked things over. Kerry could with ease fall over something that wasn't even there. But not Anna. Kim's eyes swivelled to Kerry, who was busy rattling knives and forks.

"Forks on the *left*, Kerry."

"Yes, I know. Oh — sorry. Left." Kerry rearranged the cutlery. Kim sighed. Kerry was perfectly intelligent. Kim knew that. But — the fact was, she still muddled left and right, however often she was told. And it was useless telling her 'You write with your right hand and the left is the one that's left' because Kerry never did write. She played noughts and crosses sometimes, or dots, or snakes, but then she seemed equally happy to use either hand. She seemed to pick one at random. Which was really very clever — ambidextrous. Kerry *was* clever. There was nothing wrong with her at all — if there had been, Kim, who knew her better than anybody, would certainly have detected it. Anybody could confuse left and right. Kim often had to stop and think before she could remember which way was east and which west. This was just the same thing. As soon as Kerry got settled at school, she'd learn like lightning.

"There's something wrong with this," Anna said plaintively.

"Let's see." Frances turned the grill down and went to look. "Oh dear." The Cremilite was, at present, neither creamy nor light. It was a nasty, bitty, lumpy pink mess. Solid undissolved globs of powder floated defiantly.

"I've been beating it for *ages*. It says two *minutes*." Anna looked again at the picture, and at her own effort. Well, it wasn't *her* fault.

"It *shouldn't* go like that." Frances frowned, puzzled. Anna had been beating it properly; the milk was O.K.; there must indeed be something wrong with the Cremilite.

"You'll have to do the Baked Alaska, after all."

"*Stupid* thing," Anna said crossly, meaning Kim and the Cremilite, both. "I'm going to watch for Mum." She marched to the door, followed by Kerry, who went upstairs to fetch her hamster, Cheeky. It was time for Cheeky's evening constitutional.

"If she was the cook, we'd all starve to death." Kim wandered over to examine the abandoned pudding. "Oh, look at this. She didn't even bother to read the instructions. You're supposed to pour the milk in first, and beat in the powder *gradually*. No wonder it's gone disgusting. What a waste." Suddenly, perversely, Kim found she wanted to salvage the hated goo. Perhaps if she whisked it for long enough, with the rotary whisk . . .

"I suppose it's worth a try," Frances said, watching as Kim set grimly to work. With Kim in that mood the Cremilite would probably find itself doing as it was told. "Ah, there goes Anna out of the gate. Mum must have just got off the bus." Mrs. Tate ran the handicrafts section of Wilshires department store in nearby Thornton Cross. She finished work at five; a convenient and surprisingly efficient bus service generally got her to the end of Chisholm Avenue by twenty past.

The front door slammed; Anna danced in, tugging at her mother's shopping basket. There ought to be something in it for her. Mrs. Tate popped her head round the kitchen door. She was a tall woman, with thick chestnut hair. Kim had inherited the height, Kerry the hair, Frances had her mother's practicality and Anna her self-confidence, but none of them had what Kim called her Presence. Mrs. Tate had an air about her as if she were Somebody. Had she been born a couple of generations earlier she would have been; her family, the Rentons, had in those days been extremely wealthy. But her grandfather Joshua Renton had been a one-man financial disaster. He invested the Renton fortunes in the stock market, backing his hunches with typical Renton confidence. Soon the Renton fortunes ceased to exist. All that had been passed down to his granddaughter Julia Renton was a collection of jewellery, thriftily hoarded by Joshua's wife Elizabeth, who was not a Renton and had little confidence, particularly not in her husband's hunches.

"I'm just going to sit in the other room till tea's ready," Mrs. Tate said, doing a double-take at the sight of Kim, industriously whisking. "Yes, Anna, I remembered your comic . . . what's for tea, Frances? . . . Kerry, there's a hamster on your neck . . . Anna, will you *wait* . . . did somebody say *creosote*? . . . Frances, are we all right for bread? . . . no, Anna, you may not stay up till half past-ten to see the end of the film — I don't care if it *is* James Bond . . ."

Frances, of course, did the cheese on toast to perfection, the cheese browned in speckles, melting and oozing over the sides of the thick pieces of toast. "Why keep a daughter and bake yourself?" Mrs. Tate murmured, not for the first time, as she took her seat next to Kerry. Anna muttered something about baking Alaska, and gave Kim a Look. Kim Looked back.

"Now don't you two start," said their mother. "I've only just got in."

"Mum, you know it's holidays."

"The fact had not escaped me, Anna."

"Well, I haven't got to get up early in the morning, have I? Don't you think . . ."

"Anna, under no circumstances are you staying up to watch the end of that film!"

"What sort of day did you have?" Frances asked hastily,

since Anna looked far from ready to drop the subject.

"Well. Little Linda managed to add up three four-figure numbers. A great day in the history of Wilshires." Linda was Mrs. Tate's newest assistant, just sixteen. "Otherwise — very quiet. Too quiet, actually. That nasty little shop in the Broadway is getting a lot of our trade." That nasty little shop, a specialist arts and crafts store, had opened three months previously. It was called Crafty. "They've got such a huge range of stock. We need to expand — start selling rug canvasses, macramé string, lampshade kits, as well as wool and cotton and tapestry threads. That's just not enough these days. Mr. Wilshire wants to see me on Wednesday. I'll have a word with him about it then. Frances, darling, that was lovely."

Kim smiled dangerously, and rose to her feet. "And now, folks, for the taste of real strawberries and cream . . ."

"Oh *no*." Anna wrinkled her nose with distaste. "Mum, she's going to give us the Cremilite and it's gone *revolting*. Well, I don't want any. I can't eat that."

"Fine," Kim said, pulling a tray from the fridge. "I'll have yours, then, and that'll be right. I somehow fancy Cremilite today." Anna retired behind her comic, wanting nothing to do with it, and thus missed the transformation scene. Kim had outdone the picture on the packet. Not only had she whisked the Cremilite smooth and tipped it into the little individual glass dishes, she had also decorated the tops with hundreds and thousands, and a glacé cherry in the centre.

"Good gracious," said Mrs. Tate.

"*Told* you," chirruped Anna, not looking up. It was none of her responsibility; Kim had taken it over, and Anna always rather enjoyed Kim's culinary disasters. *She* would not offend her delicate and discerning palate by *tasting* the stuff. She . . . "*Oh!*"

"It turned out rather well, in the end," Kim said tranquilly, licking her spoon. Anna's jaw dropped. Oh, it wasn't fair! It was mean! It was doubly terrible; Kim had succeeded where she had failed — and it looked so lovely and the others were eating it all up and there wasn't any for her! "Something wrong?" asked Kim. Mrs. Tate looked suspiciously from her eldest daughter to her youngest; as usual, there was a battle going on under the comparatively civilized surface, and Kim was clearly, at this stage, winning.

"I am *not hungry*," Anna said. "I am *going to my room*."

"Yes, dear," murmured Mrs. Tate as Anna shut the door behind her. "You *may* be excused. Kim . . ."

"And I was just going to offer her mine," Kim said sadly. Mrs. Tate raised a dubious eyebrow. "No, truly I was. I don't like the stuff much, really. She's welcome to it. But she did *say* she didn't want any." This, of course, was perfectly true; all the same, Mrs. Tate wasn't happy.

"Actually," she said, "I'm not too keen on it myself, this Cremilite. I tell you what, Kim; we'll put what's left of ours into one dish and Madame Butterfly can have the lot when she comes down. Then she'll have had more than anybody . . ."

Kim agreed. "There's one of those huge bananas left in the fruit bowl in the other room. Shall we have that instead? Half each?"

"That's more like it," Mrs. Tate said, pouring herself another cup of tea. All the Tates were very fond of bananas. The banana was fetched and disposed of; Frances and Kerry ate on, placid observers.

It took some time to persuade Anna to come down, but calls of "We've *got* something for you" could not be indefinitely resisted. "But I don't want that!" she said, when presented with the Cremilite. "Nasty leftovers all scraped together! It's horrible! It looks awful!" It did, rather.

"Look, darling, suppose you find yourself something else, then. Because I'm getting rather tired of Cremilite."

Anna recognized a certain warning tone in her mother's

voice. She considered. "Well . . .I know! I'll have that lovely big banana that's in the bowl on the sideboard. I'll have it cut up with sugar and Ideal Milk." They were sure to let her have the last banana, after she'd been so shabbily treated . . .

"Oh dear," said her mother, casting a malevolent glare at Kim, who gazed back at her with injured innocence, and rose, bristling with virtue, to do the washing up.

Anna saw the end of the James Bond film.

2

NOBODY QUITE REMEMBERED EXACTLY when the trouble
had started with Kerry. At first she had seemed to like
school well enough. But then, more and more frequently,
she began to feel ill on school mornings. She had stomach
aches, headaches; she developed mysterious pains.

It was all very puzzling to Mrs. Tate. Kerry was such an
unlikely malingerer. But the pains never materialized at
week-ends, so malingering she must be. Kerry, unwell or
not, was sent to school. It was at this point that she began
actually to be sick. She was sick first thing in the morning; if
forced to go to school she was sick there. Time and time
again she had to be fetched home before lunchtime, wan and
tearful. She lost her appetite. She looked haunted. It was
very distressing for everybody.

The authorities stepped in. Kerry was missing great
chunks of school now, spending the days at her
grandmother's house. Both Kerry and her grandmother
liked this arrangement very much, but of course it could not
be allowed to continue. Children must be educated. Kerry
began to do the rounds. She saw child psychologists,
educational psychologists, and a variety of medical
specialists. Her eyesight and hearing were tested; both were
excellent. She seemed intelligent, although since she

strongly resisted all kinds of intelligence test, it was not easy
to tell. The experts gave their diagnosis: a clear case of school
phobia. Now, all they had to do was to find the cause, and
the problem could be speedily solved.

But the reason remained elusive. The experts had talked to
Kerry's teachers; they had talked to Mrs. Tate, to Mr. Tate
and to Kerry, alone and in all possible permutations. Mrs.
Tate came home and talked to Kim. Kim talked to Frances
and to David. A Mrs. Lucas came to the house and talked to
everybody. The only person who didn't talk was Kerry; she
wasn't saying anything. Even Kim could get little out of her.
When pressed, she shrank miserably into her chair, eyes
huge and pleading.

It was just one more big worry for Mrs. Tate, who had a
great many already. If Kerry didn't go to school, she, her
mother, was breaking the law. But if complying with the law
meant upsetting a small child to the point of making her
ill . . . this past term, Kerry had been to school on no more
than twelve occasions. But, like Kim, Mrs. Tate was
basically an optimist. Kerry was to see a new psychologist
this coming Friday; this one, surely, would get through to
her. And there would be an end to the dismal school
mornings, with Anna coming downstairs half asleep and
irritable: "Mum, Kerry's being sick again . . ."

It was all so different in the holidays. Kim swore that she
could tell in her very first second of consciousness whether
or not it was a schoolday. The whole atmosphere of the
house was completely changed.

"You're looking very thoughtful." Mrs. Tate came into
the kitchen, ready to leave for work, all early-morning
efficiency. "Now, Kim, your father should be here at ten
thirty for these two — so be sure they're ready and
waiting — and tell Frances I'll bring the potatoes." Frances
was not an early riser. "Bye, Kerry — bye, Anna . . . no, I
won't forget to bring another bottle of lemonade . . ." Kim

watched as her mother left the house, cool, crisp and elegant in white cotton. She wondered if she would ever look like that, and decided no, not in a million years. Kim didn't mostly bother much about her appearance. Some of the girls in her class were forever peering into mirrors, and daubing shiny gunge on their eyelids when they thought they could get away with it. Mrs. Hanrahan, 2K's form mistress, told them often and bluntly what she thought of them, but it seemed to make no difference. Kim thought they were daft wasting money on those silly tiny pots of eye shadow, or whatever. You were stuck with what you looked like. Green eyelids didn't change it, they just told the world that you were worried about it. It was already obvious that Frances and Anna would be pretty, Kerry would be interesting-looking — and the most Kim could hope for was the upper range of ordinary. At the rate she was growing, she'd be in the upper range of anything . . .

It was just eight; she switched the radio on for the weather forecast that would follow the news. The car workers' strike had entered its second week . . . renewed hostilities in the Middle East . . . light aircraft crashed in East Anglia . . .

"And now the Thames Area weather — and it's good news — another hot, sunny day with temperatures reaching eighty-five degrees in the afternoon. So get your swimsuits out. This is Radio Thames, and you're tuned to your cuddly breakfast show — Bill Maloney, with all the sounds around — in half an hour we'll be going over to Kidsline, but right now here's the Police . . ."

"*Cuddly*," Kim said scornfully. They got stupider every day.

"I *like* cuddly," said Anna.

"How the hell can you like cuddly? It's just a *word*."

"Well, I like it. And shut up. I like the Police too."

"Pardon me for existing." Trust Anna to pop up with the dawn, fresh as a daisy, after her late-night viewing. She

25

should have been tucked up in bed having nightmares about guns and lasers and villains with lethal bowler hats. "I'm going next door for a moment."

"What for? To see David?"

"Oh no. I just thought I'd sweep the Holders' chimney for them." If sarcasm was the lowest form of wit, then it was very appropriate for squashing the lowest form of human life.

"Oh, it's you," said Bryony.

"Can I speak to David, please?"

"What do you want him for?"

"I thought we might go to the swimming baths," Kim said, only just resisting the temptation to ask to speak to the organ grinder, not the monkey.

"He can't," Bryony said triumphantly. "We've got *people* coming." She looked at Kim as if to imply that 'people' was a category from which she would certainly exclude her.

"What? But he said yesterday, about going out — that we might go cycling if it wasn't too hot . . ."

"I can't help that. He knew quite well."

"Look, can I *speak* to him, please, Bryony? You can have him straight back."

Bryony glowered and withdrew. David appeared a moment later.

"*Sorry*. It just went clear out of my head. It's cousins; they don't come very often, and I have to *be* here."

"Which cousins are those?"

"The Yorkshire ones. Rupert and Rebecca. Deadly. Boring. It's very easy to forget about them. Rebecca's not so bad. But Rupert — he's grown into his name."

"Never stood a chance, really."

"Not really," agreed David. "Was Bri-Nylon particularly awful?"

"Not particularly. Just about average. Well — perhaps a

26

little worse."

"We're in a *frightful* bad mood this morning. We're packing to go to Camilla's and we haven't got a *clue* what we might need to wear. And of course we can't ring up and *ask* Camilla because that would be admitting that we didn't know . . ."

Stupid great gumboil, Kim thought, vaulting back over the wall. Well, that was that. She *could* go swimming on her own, of course, but it happened to be one of the few things that she only really enjoyed when she had company.

Anna had turned the radio up, and had woken Frances.

"Are you going out with David?"

"He can't," Kim said shortly.

"Haven't you got *any* other friends except David? I," said Anna, "have got *fourteen* friends."

"Only fourteen? When I was your age I had sixty-eight." Kim did have friends — she was well liked by most people in her class — but no really close ones. She'd never once had a Special Best Friend, like Frances had Janice; nor did she much want one, having heard what some people said about Best Friend, behind Best Friend's back. In 2K alliances were formed and broken with alarming rapidity, and relations with former Best Friends were seldom sweet. Kim reckoned she was well out of it; at least she kept on speaking terms with everybody. And she'd rather have David than any Best Friend. Blow it, David *was* her best friend, without the capital letters, which was different, and better.

"If you want to go somewhere," Frances said, "I don't mind waiting in till Dad comes. Or do you want to see him?"

Well, she *did* — but he'd only be stopping for a moment. It wasn't worth staying in for; she was, in any case, spending the whole afternoon with him on Sunday. "No. Thanks, Frances. I think I'll go to the library."

"Kim! You *can't* go today when I can't come too. You

27

always take me to the library. You know you do."

"Well, I'm sorry about that, Anna, but my books need changing. You can't expect me not to go just because you're doing something else, can you?" Anna, plainly, could. "I'll take you another day. I promise. The very first day you want to go. Want anything, Kerry?"

"Um — yes. The pig and the spider."

"*Charlotte's Web*," translated Kim. "Right. Now, you two have a nice time. O.K.? I'll see you when you get back."

Anna loved the library. Her behaviour there was always immaculate, and she was a great favourite with Paula, the children's librarian. It was a newly built library, three storeys high, with a large mosaic mural over the entrance, and puzzling pieces of modern statuary in the aisles and on the staircases. Kim had christened them all; her favourite was 'Park Bench Doing the Tango with Lamppost'.

Kim always had to select two sets of books, her own and Kerry's. She read to Kerry every single day; it kept her from missing too much. When Kerry began to read herself she'd be able to take up from where Kim had left off. They got through at least two books a week, yet Kerry always knew instantly if Kim made a mistake and brought the same book twice. She stopped her in the first paragraph. Kim couldn't possibly have remembered the openings of so many books; Kerry must have a phenomenal memory. Some books, such as *Charlotte's Web*, she liked very much, and requested again and again.

Kim chose three books for herself: a tale of darkest skulduggery in the streets of Victorian London, a book called *Athletics for Everybody* which might, just possibly, contain some bright ideas as to how she might practise the high jump without access to any sports equipment, and a detective story.

"I've something for Kerry," said Paula. "*Tales of the River Folk*. And ask her when she's coming to see me, will you? Tell her she's hurting my feelings. And where's Anna today?"

"Going out with Dad, both of them."

"How's the book coming along?"

Kim wished she knew. "I'll try to find out on Sunday. He's been working terribly hard at it." She stayed talking to Paula for some time. Then she stopped to look at an exhibition of photographs in the entrance hall, just behind 'Three-Legged Cello Knitting a Sock' — so, since it wasn't hurrying weather, it was twenty past eleven by the time she got home to find Anna and Kerry still there, fidgety and cross, and her father, obviously, not coming.

"He's forgotten," Frances said. It was possible. It was even probable; he did forget things. He'd forgotten to telephone on Frances' last birthday; he was continually forgetting to send money. But never before had he actually failed to turn up. "Shall we phone him? He could still take them for the afternoon."

"*No*." Because if he'd forgotten it could only be because he was lost in his writing. It might be the most important point yet. He might just be unblocking a serious writer's blockage. On no account must he be disturbed at such a time; it might hold up the book for months. The sooner he finished it, the sooner he'd be back.

"All right," said Frances, surprised. "Just a suggestion. How about this, then — I'll drop them off at Gran's, on the way to Janice's house . . ."

"We are *here* , you know," said Anna. "You could ask *us* what we want to do. And I don't want to go to Gran's." The trouble with Gran was, not only was Kerry her favourite, but she insisted on saying so, practically every time she saw them. "Hello, Kim — Frances, you're looking lovely — and Anna — and my Kerry! How's my favourite?" It was just sickening. Mrs. Tate thought so, too. She was always telling Gran off about it when she thought they weren't listening. Gran was Mr. Tate's mother; she and Mrs. Tate didn't get on at all. Nor was this Gran's only failing. She never did meals the right way. Her chips were the wrong shape, her plates the wrong size, her baked beans the wrong brand. Her orange squash had nasty bits floating in it. No, Anna wasn't going to Gran's.

"They might as well stay," Kim said. "I don't think Mum'd want us to dump them on Gran without any warning. And I wasn't going anywhere, particularly."

"Really? Well, I tell you what," Frances said generously, "I'll stay in as well. I don't mind not seeing Janice today."

"Why don't you ask her round here? She *never* comes round, these days." Frances shook her head. "Frances, why not? Our house is just as big as hers. So's our garden. Why doesn't she come?"

"It's just that we're used to doing what we do there," Frances said, vaguely, and would say no more.

Kim had another attack of virtue in the afternoon, and decided to give the front room a proper cleaning. She hoovered the carpet, washed the windows, scrubbed the skirting, polished the table, brushed the chair covers and dusted everything dustable, with the radio playing loudly all the while, and wearing nothing but a bathing costume. The bathing costume lent a whole new dimension to the process; it didn't feel like cleaning at all. Frances found her stretched out on the hearth-rug, sorting through the unlikely collection of items she had unearthed from beneath the seat cushions of the settee and armchairs. "*Mind my nice clean carpet*," said Kim.

Frances was helpless with laughter. You do look so funny! Have you seen yourself? You're filthy!"

"*I* may be filthy. The *room* is clean. See what I've found. Thirty pounds in Monopoly money. Six pieces of Lego. Half a digestive biscuit. A doll's left arm. And, look, my school

30

"Are you happy there?"

"Yes, thanks."

"There you are, Anna. That was Kim's school report. *This*" — she opened the envelope — "is just a list of facts and figures. Number of times late. Average age of class. Important things like that."

"But was she top of her class?"

"That's for Kim to tell you, if she wants to."

"I was second," said Kim. She supposed she might have been top, if she'd really pulled out all the stops. But it wasn't worth it. First, second — it didn't make much difference.

"Meaningless," said her mother. "The others might all be monkeys." It wasn't likely, since they were the top stream, but Kim didn't argue. She wholly approved. Not many people were lucky enough to have mothers with such a sensible attitude. Lucy Turner's parents went through their three children's reports with them, line by line, in public, at a ghastly gathering which they called a Turner Family Conference. And at Christmas they sent out special cards with a photograph of themselves on the front, and, written underneath, 'The Turner Family Christmas Card'. If Kim had had a family like that she'd have run away, years ago.

Anna went out to watch the television, trying to work out if Kim had come well or badly out of all that. She switched on to ITV, so as not to miss any advertisements, and caught the second half of an ad for a new hamburger restaurant. But that was the last one. Anna frowned. It was so annoying, the way they kept interrupting the ads with programmes. However, in the next commercial break she was rewarded with a Cremilite ad. She leaned forward in intense concentration, mouthing the words silently, and joined in softly with the Cremilite song . . . 'Creamy, dreamy Cremilite, Cremikids are always right! Orange! Banana! Chocolate! Strawberry!' Each Cremikid shouted out the name of his or her special flavour. The pink-clad strawberry girl was the one Anna had her eye on. She was definitely the least convincing of the four. "Strawberry!" shouted Anna, and ran back into the kitchen. Kim had gone out to the roof; it was now or never.

"Mum."

"Yes, Anna?"

"I've got an idea. Will you say if you think it's a good one?"

"Certainly." Anna fell silent.

"Spit it out," Frances said encouragingly. Anna slid on to a stool, suddenly shy. They might laugh at her. She hated being laughed at more than almost anything.

"Anna wants to be a Cremikid," Kerry said unexpectedly. Anna swallowed — how in the world did *Kerry* know? — and continued hastily, before her mother could speak.

"I thought if I — if I sent a photograph of me to the man who owns Cremilite he might put me in the ad. That's all. I thought it was worth trying."

Mrs. Tate hesitated, opened her mouth, closed it again. "Anna. Why exactly do you want to be in that ad so much?"

Why? Because she wanted to be on television! There could be nothing in the world more exciting than to see yourself on the screen — and to know that millions of other people were seeing you too, and wishing they could be you . . . she might be recognized in the street . . .

"Anna?"

Anna said nothing. She was turning pink. Frances came to her rescue.

"You want to earn some money, don't you, Anna? We never seem to have enough. It's a good idea, really. I wouldn't have minded doing that when I was her age, Mum."

"Umm. Is that right, Anna?"

"Yes! I was talking about it . . . to Frances . . . "

"So I gather. Well, it's very good of you to show such a

33

concern for our finances. I appreciate that. But that's not the way advertisements work, Anna. The Cremilite people wouldn't be the ones who choose the children. They hire advertising agencies to do all that sort of thing."

"Then couldn't I send a photo to the agency?"

"Anna, all those children you see on television come from stage schools. Really they do. Every one of them. They're trained, you see. They know what they're doing. So that's where the casting people always go when they want children. The general public just aren't involved. I'm sorry, darling, really."

"Did you say a stage school? A school on a stage? Where is it?"

"You've never heard of stage schools? There are quite a few of them. They train children for careers in show business generally — acting, and singing and dancing — all on top of ordinary lessons. I should think it's terribly hard work."

"What children? Just any children?"

"I suppose they have to pass some sort of audition or interview before they get in. It would be pointless taking children with no aptitude."

"The Josephine Priestley School is a stage school, isn't it?" Frances said. "The one on the corner of Barker's Lane."

Josephine Priestley? But that was practically around the corner! Anna had often seen children going in and out. They looked absolutely ordinary.

"That's right," said Mrs. Tate. "Quite a number of the children in television serials and so forth come from Josephine Priestley."

"Then — Mum — can I go there?" Anna jumped to her feet and hopped with excitement. She could start next term. From September she would be one of the élite, the special few. She would pass any audition! If only she'd known about this before! It was terrible to think of the two wasted years. "Please say I can! I want to go there more than anything in the world!" A school of acting and singing and television commercials — it would be paradise. And so near to home! It was *meant*.

Mrs. Tate was looking startled. "But Anna, you must know that I couldn't possibly afford the fees. Only state schools are free, you know."

"But there must be money!" Whenever Anna wanted something badly enough, she eventually got it. If her mother couldn't or wouldn't find the money, she asked her father when she saw him, and *he* gave it to her. But not, apparently, this time.

"Anna, it's completely out of the question. You've no idea what private education costs. The fees would be enough to feed the four of you for a year. I'm very sorry. But as I was given the impression that you only wanted to do this at all to *earn* some money, I think you'd be wise to leave it at that."

Oh, it was beastly. It was meaner than mean. If you wanted to be on television you had to be *rich*. Was that fair? It wasn't Anna's fault if they weren't. People shouldn't *have* four children if they couldn't afford them. If her parents had waited, and just had her, there would be four times as much money to spend on her, and then she'd surely have been able to go to the Josephine Priestley School. She didn't *want* three sisters. Well — perhaps just Frances. There would still be four times as much money because Frances would see how talented and how deserving Anna was, and would ask that her share be spent on Anna.

But that couldn't happen. So she'd just have to think of something else, that was all. And, in the meantime, she'd look very woebegone, and, more than likely, she'd be allowed to stay up until late again. There were always compensations.

3

"I'VE SENT ANNA TO bed," said Mrs. Tate, as Kim came in from the roof, where she and David had been holding a pleasant inquest on the visit of the unlovely Rupert and Rebecca. "She was getting on my nerves. All wounded and hard done by. I had enough of that last night. Kerry's gone up too; Frances is in the bath. Your father rang, Kim. He just remembered. He hopes they weren't too disappointed. He'll see you on Sunday, twoish."

"Did he forget because he was writing?"

"We didn't go into that," Mrs. Tate said shortly. "Kim. I have to talk to you. Will you come down after you've finished reading to Kerry?"

"About Dad?"

"No, not about Dad. Don't look so worried. It's nothing terrible."

It must, Kim decided, be Kerry. On that subject, her mother had taken her completely into her confidence; perhaps it was too much worry for any one person to cope with. When she came downstairs, leaving Kerry asleep and Anna sulking — something, obviously, had happened while she was with David — Kim found two mugs on the kitchen table, and her mother boiling milk for hot chocolate.

"Sit down — it's nearly ready." Mrs. Tate spooned chocolate into the milk, stirred and poured. For the duration of the chocolate Kim would be an adult. She picked the skin from the top of the chocolate, draped it over the side of the mug, and waited.

"The psychologist I'm taking Kerry to see on Friday morning. I've been talking to him on the phone. He wants you to go too."

"Me? Why?"

"You know her so well, darling. He thinks it may help him to talk to you."

"Oh. Well. All right." It was a shocking waste of one of the few mornings remaining before David went away, and Kim didn't like psychologists at all . . . But she didn't really have any choice. Kerry would be pleased, anyhow.

"And Kim — I have to warn you — you may not like the questions he asks. He'll probably ask you things that you feel are absolutely none of his business. You will answer, won't you? You won't bite his head off?"

It sounded horrendous. "Oh, I'll answer." But not, necessarily, truthfully . . .

"It's hateful, Kim. Every time — and God knows there've been enough times — every single time they start asking those personal questions my hackles rise. And I know you. You'll feel the same way. But you have to grit your teeth and remind yourself that they are actually trying to help Kerry. We *have* to co-operate with them. They're holding all the cards, you see? They've got the power. They *could* take Kerry away."

"They could *what*?"

"Kim, I don't for one moment think the possibility has even entered their minds. But it is, theoretically, within their powers to . . . Kim, are you all right? You've gone terribly pale."

"I'm all right," Kim said after a moment. "You just gave

me a shock, that's all." She didn't feel all right, though. She felt quite sick. Beastly, interfering authorities . . .

"Kim, they won't *do* it. They're there to help people like Kerry, not to break up families. I wish I hadn't said anything now."

Kim looked marginally more cheerful. "So do I wish you hadn't. Who is this psychologist anyway? Not Mrs. Lucas this time?"

"No, it's a man — a Mr. Gilbert. He's never seen Kerry before. That's why I'm so hopeful. Whenever she sees anybody new, I always think, this'll be the one."

"You wouldn't imagine, with all those kids going round nicking things and mugging old ladies, that they'd have time to bother with someone like Kerry. I mean, it's *their* beastly school she doesn't want to go to. It's *their* fault really."

"That's an interesting point of view." Mrs. Tate grinned ruefully. "But I wouldn't mention it to Mr. Gilbert, just the same. Kim — do you still have no idea at all? I know she talks to you, as much as she ever talks to anybody. I wonder sometimes — if I didn't have to be out at work all day — if I'd spent more time with her perhaps she'd have said something to me by now — oh well. I've always had a feeling that when there's a breakthrough it won't be any of the experts that makes it; it'll be you."

"She talks to me," said Kim, "but not about that." The only theory that Kim had put together, built up from a number of tiny, vague hints over the years, was that for some reason Kerry couldn't *manage* at school. And she'd been away so much, missed out on such a lot of work, that now she was beginning to think herself retarded. She hadn't put it like that, of course. But Kim knew. And the words 'educationally subnormal' always made her feel — well, uneasy. *She* knew it wasn't true; it was unfortunate, though, that Kerry's cleverness was not of a sort that could be readily appreciated by other people, by outsiders. What did they think of her? What did the authorities have written down in their files? "Mum? Kerry *is* bright, isn't she? You know that. She isn't — there's no way she could be sort of backward without us *realizing*."

"Of course she's not backward. I'll tell you what I think. I think she's a late developer. Nothing wrong with that. So was Churchill."

"*Was* he?"

"And Einstein, I think. So I've got every confidence in the world that she'll catch up. And maybe she'll never be much inclined towards academic subjects. What do *you* see her doing?"

"When she's grown up? Working with animals."

"Exactly. So the Three Rs won't necessarily be the be all and end all. She'll catch up, anyway. People do. My brother Jack could hardly read at *eleven*. He learned. People develop at different rates. My grandmother Elizabeth was the same. She learned. So that's not what worries me. Kerry'll be fine. It's just the pressure from the authorities that's so awful."

Kim nodded. She'd seen photographs of Great-Grandmother Elizabeth, and a very shrewd lady she looked, too. And Uncle Jack, a huge man with a ginger beard and a habit of swinging small children in the air above his head, was most certainly not backward. He had his own shop, an electrical business. It spoke well for Kerry's future.

"Don't you want your chocolate?"

"Yes, but I'm waiting for it to cool off. It's such a warm evening. I think it's been even hotter today than yesterday."

"Drink it cold. Pretend it's a milk shake."

"That's what I'm going to do. Only it keeps making new skins," said Kim, fishing out another.

"You're sapping its strength," her mother said. "There's nothing quite like a mug of skinned cold hot chocolate. *Almost* as good as Cremilite."

Frances was lying on top of her bed, with the window wide open, her long strawberry-blonde hair tumbling over the pillow.

"I had my bath too hot," she said mournfully as Kim padded in. She felt as if she had been lightly boiled, and was still steaming.

"And we've been making hot chocolate," said Kim. "We must all be mad." She pulled her pyjamas on and flopped back on to her own bed. "I've heard that in the desert it gets very cold at night." Frances appeared totally indifferent to this piece of information. "What's the matter with Anna?"

"Promise you won't tease her?"

"I shan't say a *word*."

Frances explained.

"Oh my God. Stage school. And we're only just managing to get by as it is. She ought to know better."

"I don't think it's particularly stage school that she wants. She just thinks she does, at the moment. There are loads of other things that would do just as well."

Kim thought about this. "She's never said anything about seriously wanting to train for the stage. I reckon she just sees the Josephine Priestley School as Instant Fame. Walk through the door and somebody points a movie camera at you. What she actually *wants*," Kim said with heavy scorn, "is to be *seen*. Can you imagine that?"

"She is pretty, you know."

"She's *cute*. I'll tell you what she looks like, Frances. You know those Disney films? The short ones, on TV. There's a kid and a pet skunk, and the skunk does something awful like eating Grandma so the parents throw it out, and the kid loves the skunk like crazy so it breaks its heart, and then the skunk saves the kid's life so the parents forgive it, and a voice says: 'Billy sure learned a lot from that skunk' and the kid and the skunk walk off together into the sunset. Sometimes

40

it's a raccoon. Well, the kids always look the same — blonde, freckly and *cute*. Like Anna. She's a Disney kid. Only don't tell her, for God's sake. She'd think it was a compliment."

Frances was enthralled. "But, Kim, I can't imagine Anna acting with a skunk. Even at the zoo, she doesn't go very near the animals' cages."

"Anna," said Kim, "goes to the Zoo so that the *animals* can look at *her*." The curtain rippled; a slight breeze was rising, and soon it grew cooler, and they fell asleep.

Thanks to her rash promise to Anna, Kim spent Wednesday morning in exactly the same way as she had Tuesday morning: in the library. Kerry went along too, and contrived to trip over the base of 'Ballerina Melting into Saucepan'. Neither Kerry nor the statue was harmed, but a foul grumpy man stopped and said something sour about children not being allowed into libraries if they were going to run about and make nuisances of themselves — did they think they were in a playground? "She *wasn't* running," Kim said furiously, helping Kerry to her feet. "She *tripped*." Anna had moved away, dissociating herself from them.

"And not before time," said Paula. "What have *you* been doing with yourself?" They fell into a long discussion about Speedy, and Cheeky the hamster, and Paula's West Highland terrier Hamish. Anna found this dull, and went off to choose her books. Kim had brought back *Athletics for Everybody*, which had proved totally useless. She looked about vaguely for something to take in its place. She seemed to have already read everything worth reading. Why were there never any books about all the things that so fascinated her and David — things like torture and transplant surgery . . . grisly murder . . . embalming . . . spontaneous combustion . . . this reminded her that she must tell David about the terrible Rat Torture which she had found in a book in the adults' section *That* was the sort of book they could do with in the children's library. It would bring the kids in in droves. It would solve the literacy problem overnight. She went and told Paula about it. Paula was interested, particularly in the Rat Torture, but she said that you had to be very careful, with children's books. There had once been quite a fuss about Noddy's disrespectful treatment of Mr. Plod the policeman, and the Rat Torture, though obviously far less serious, might not be too well received. But she was grateful for the tip. If Kim would give her the title of the book, she rather thought she'd have a look at it herself.

"Tell me about the Rat Torture," Anna said for the seventh time.

"Certainly not." Frances had allowed Kim to help prepare the salad; she was slicing hard-boiled eggs with a knife (the egg slicer was lost) and making rather a mess of the yolk; it kept crumbling. "You're *far* too young. It would give you nightmares."

"I *never* have nightmares. Look what you're doing to that egg. It's gone horrible. I'm not having that one. It's *nasty*."

"It's *crumbled*. If you haven't got the stomach for a crumbled egg yolk, you certainly couldn't bear to hear the Rat Torture."

"I can!" Anna scented a bargain. "Kim, if I have that egg, the one you've just spoiled, *then* will you tell me?"

"No," said Kim. At that moment Mrs. Tate came in from work, and Anna, who was just working herself up to be very indignant indeed, fell silent, because it was obvious, even to her, that something was dreadfully wrong. Mrs. Tate looked furious. Livid. And worried, and upset, all mixed up together, but mainly furious. Frances turned from the slab, her mouth opening with a cheerful 'Hi' — she saw, and the 'Hi' died unspoken. Kerry sidled over and stood by Kim.

"Well. There's no point beating about the bush. You might as well know. I saw Mr. Wilshire today. The handicrafts department isn't going to be expanded. It's going to be closed down. And I've lost my job."

"He's *sacked* you?"

"I've been made redundant. It is *slightly* better. I'll get some redundancy pay, and good references. But I'm still out of a job. Four kids to support, and Mr. Wilshire really doesn't see *how* he can keep me on. Terrific."

"But why?" Kim was stunned. Her mother had been working at Wilshires, first part-time, then full-time, for years and years now. Surely they couldn't *do* this?

"O.K. I'll explain. You know there's a recession hitting the country at the moment? Well, it's also hitting Mr. Wilshire. He's decided he'll have to close down three departments that aren't paying their way. And, thanks to that nasty little shop in the Broadway, Handicrafts is top of the death list. All our customers are switching to Crafty. The department's like a tomb. We can't compete. Frances, do you think I could have a cup of tea?" Frances scuttled to the kettle.

"But couldn't he have given you another job? Moved you to one of the other departments?"

"Bull's eye, Kim. Of course he could. The heads of three other departments are coming up for retirement. I could have replaced any one of them. I know it. He knows I know it. Imagine what a pleasant little chat we had. Oh yes, he did offer me a part-time job in Furnishings. Knowing full well that I have to work full-time. The truth of it is, he's rather glad to see the back of me."

"Why?" Frances was horrified. "You're ever so good at your job."

"Two reasons, actually. I have, in the past, been known to disagree with him. Mr. Wilshire doesn't like that at all. He likes people to say yes sir, no sir, three bags full sir, unless you'd rather have four sir. And it's so *very* inconvenient for him when I have to take a morning off, say, to take my daughter to see a psychologist, or if I ask for time off to stay with two other daughters who happen to have chicken pox rather badly. *He* can't help it if I'm struggling to bring up four children on my own. He hoped I'd understand that it has never been his policy to take matters like that into consideration. So I thanked him kindly for his compassion, and we decided that, all things considered, I might as well leave as soon as possible. My holiday was due to start on Monday. It still will; I just shan't be going back afterwards."

Nobody knew what to say. It was Anna who eventually broke the silence.

"What's going to happen to Little Linda?"

"She's being transferred to Kitchenware."

"Did she cry when you told her you were going?"

"Not exactly. She said: 'Yes, Mrs. Tate. That's a shame, isn't it, Mrs. Tate. Can I take my tea break now, Mrs. Tate?' " Suddenly she began to laugh rather wildly. "Don't all look so miserable! It's not the end of the world. I'll get another job. Right — I know what. We're going to have a party. I'm going to the off licence to get a bottle of wine and lots of Coke — salted peanuts — put the salad in the fridge, we'll have that tomorrow. I'm fetching fish and chips. We're going to celebrate!"

"Celebrate what?" Frances asked, dazed.

"Celebrate the glorious fact that I'm not working for Mr. Wilshire any more. Come *on*, you lot. Smile! We'll get through this. We'll show them."

Mrs. Tate was riotously gay throughout the party, and Kim, tiptoeing downstairs at midnight, quite unable to sleep, was not one bit surprised to find her sitting at the table, crying her eyes out. "Don't go," she said in a snuffly voice. "I've just finished."

"Is it *that* bad?" Kim said presently.

44

"It's pretty bad, Kim. Jobs are so hard to come by, these days. Especially for someone of my age, with no real training for anything that's likely to help. Oh, I'll find something. But it may take a while. Till then — I'll have to draw unemployment money. The dole. Doesn't it sound ghastly! Still, when you're responsible for four children you can't afford to be proud."

"You'll always be proud," said Kim, "whatever you have to do."

"Thank you." Her mother flashed her a sudden, warm smile. "I'll remember that."

"Is Dad forgetting to send money?" Kim asked, not wanting to ask, but needing to know.

"He's sent nothing for three months now. I sometimes wonder if he's even working *part*-time any longer. Well, I suppose he must be or he couldn't afford to live."

"If only he'd get the book finished." Everything would be so different, then. "I know it wouldn't be published straight away, but if he'd only finish it he could come home and do his proper job again, and there'd be *plenty* of money . . ."

Mrs. Tate usually responded to this sort of thing with murmurs of agreement. But this time she said: "Finished? I doubt if he's even started it."

"Mum! Of course he's started it. I've seen it! He's done tons already, tons and tons. Well, it looks like tons."

"Kim? Are you sure? Then — why haven't you ever said so before?"

"I thought you knew — Mum, I thought he'd have told you how he was getting on."

"Since the day he left," said her mother, "he has never once mentioned the book to me. I'd started wondering if he ever meant there to be a book at all."

"But — that was what he went for!" Just after Christmas it had been, when he went — two Christmasses ago, now. Kim hadn't really believed it, not deep down, until the next

45

morning when she saw his empty place at the table, and knew that it was true. He'd spent the night at his new flat; he'd really done it. He had told the four of them about it one afternoon in the autumn. Their mother hadn't been there. She already knew.

"I'm going to write a book," he had said. "It's something I've wanted to do very badly for a long time. Not just any book. It's going to be long, and it'll be difficult to write. But — you know my friend Michael? Well, he's an editor, and he's very keen on the book. It's going to be a best seller; it's just the sort of thing people like to read. So he's going to publish it when it's finished. But I'll need a good deal of peace and quiet. I have to read lots of other books, before I can write mine. I can't do that here with you four running about. It wouldn't be fair on you to keep asking you to hush. So I'm going away. I'm going to find a little flat and live there on my own till I've finished. And then I'll come straight back." He stopped, smiled his gentle smile, and looked at each of them in turn. "It won't be for very long. You'll all come and see me, as often as you like! And I'll come and see you. It won't be so very different, really. Your mother's going to start working full-time, like I do now, and I'll be working part-time like *she* does now. So there'll be plenty of money. And just as soon as the book comes out, we're going to be rich!"

But that hadn't happened yet, and there wasn't plenty of money — how could there be, when they had two homes to keep up now instead of one — and their mother had far too much to do, and never enough time to do it? It *was* different, very different. How could it be the same, when you had to travel ten miles to see your own father? Their visits to his flat seemed to be getting farther and farther apart, and Kerry and Anna were beginning to forget how it had been when he had lived at home. Kim hadn't forgotten. But even she couldn't help but notice how, these days, when her father came to the house he was starting to seem more like a visitor than a member of the family. He *must* finish the book soon! "I'll ask him on Sunday," she said in a rush. "I'll ask him exactly how much of it he's done and then we'll know more or less how long it'll take him to do the rest."

"Well, I wish you would." Her mother was looking startled, and very pleased. "I just had no idea, Kim. That's marvellous news." Her usual good spirits were resurfacing, rapidly. "Oh, I bet I'll get another job in no time. We'll get the papers and start job hunting. It'll be fun, you'll see. I was so bored with Handicrafts, anyhow . . ."

"I wish I could get a job. A holiday job. People *do*. And it would help."

"Oh, that's nice of you, darling! But I'm afraid you've just missed the bus. Everything that was going for the holidays is sure to have been snapped up by now. There wouldn't have been much you could have done anyway; thirteen-year-olds are only allowed to work very short hours."

"I'm nearly fourteen. I *look* fourteen." Not that it made much difference. "There must be something I can do," she said, stubbornly. "I'll have a think about it." Her mother smiled at her with deep affection. *Money,* thought Kim. Money, money, money. Making the world go round. Pieces of metal and pieces of paper. People murdered and died for it, cheated and lied for it. Workers went on strike to get more of it; Mr. Wilshire closed down departments that couldn't make enough of it. Well, the Tates would manage. They'd get by. They weren't on the breadline. And they had the Renton jewellery: locked away in a bank vault for safety, always, comfortingly, *there*. Kim had seen it twice. As a rule she wasn't particularly keen on jewellery, but this meant something — it was the Renton heritage, and eventually, she supposed, she would inherit a quarter of it. Kim Tate, heiress. Now *there* was a thought. She had, from time to

47

time, wondered about the diamond and sapphire necklace. This was by far the most valuable single item. Would she, as the eldest, be entitled to it? It would be rather nice to *have* it. Even if she didn't especially like it.

It wasn't until much later that Kim realized the full significance of what her mother had said that night. "I'd started wondering if he ever meant there to be a book at all . . ." Kim had never really been able to find out what her mother felt about the writing of this book. She rarely spoke about it. But no wonder she had been so thrilled to learn of the mounting pile of pages; if she believed he never meant there to be a book, she must have thought that, all the time, it had just been an excuse to go off and leave them for ever.

4

"COOLER TODAY," SAID DAVID, appearing in the front garden. "Coming over to Warren Hill?"

Kim paused, half in, half out of the gate, went back and leaned against the wall. "Do you mind if we don't, today? I thought I'd go odd-jobbing. I could do with a bit of extra pocket money."

David considered this for a moment, and said: "Not a bad idea. I could use some extra holiday money, come to that. Hang on a tick and I'll come with you." He vanished indoors. Kim waited, pleased but surprised. The Holder children were very rarely short of cash. Still — knocking on strangers' doors was always *much* better when there were two of you. Particularly when you were trying to part them from their money.

"This," said David, "is my anti-mugger jacket. Secret inside pocket. By the time they find it you'll have had time to walk to the police station and back."

"And you'll be lying in a pool of blood . . . d'you really think we're going to get enough to make us worth mugging?"

"No harm in hoping. I'll store the takings in the pocket and we'll split it when we've finished. O.K.?"

"O.K. Hey" — as David turned purposefully to the

right, into Broadmeadow Lane — "where are you going? What's the matter with *this* road?"

"Everybody who ever goes scrounging knows that *the* place to go is Addison Avenue. We'll make twice as much there in half the time. Raffle ticket sellers — Oxfam — carol singers — penny for the guy — they throng there in their thousands."

"Join the happy throng. I hope they've got some money left, that's all."

"The great thing about Addison Avenue is that they've *always* got money left. Kim — by the way — I'm so sorry about your mother's job."

"How the hell do you know about that?" Kim said grumpily.

"My mother saw your mother last night in the off licence. She told her. She said you were celebrating it." Mrs. Holder had been no more fooled by Mrs. Tate's gaiety than had Kim; she told David, who entirely agreed with her, that Mrs. Tate was a *superb* lady. And very courageous. "You do seem to have bad luck, Kim."

"We do not!" Kim swung round in amazement; what a peculiar thing to say. And then she remembered what David thought about her father; he saw that she remembered, and neither of them said any more about it.

They began at the beginning, with the first house. Nobody was in. "That's the catch," David said. "They all spend the summer on the Riviera."

"Let's come back at Christmas and sing carols."

"People only pay carol singers to make them go away. Why wait till Christmas? It would work just as well now. Better." They marched up the next path singing *O Come All Ye Faithful*. The door was opened by a tall, severe-looking man of about seventy.

"What's this?" David explained. "Bob a job! Ha!" He looked at Kim. "You don't look much like a Boy Scout."

"I'm a civilian," said Kim.

"Air Force," said the man, with pride. "Battle of Britain. Those were the days. What this country needs is another war!" David looked disgusted; Kim began to hum *God Rest Ye Merry, Gentlemen*, softly.

"Lawn needs mowing," said the man. "At the back. That the sort of thing you had in mind? Good. Lawnmower in the shed. Mind my wife."

"When the Russians nuke us," Kim said, "he'll die laughing." They found his wife dozing in a garden chair, plum in the middle of the lawn, which did need mowing, badly. The wife opened her eyes, and looked alarmed. David explained again.

"But the mower's broken!" she said. "It's been broken for weeks. I'd suggest that you borrowed next door's, but they've gone to the Riviera. I know what you could do, though. There's a flower-bed beyond the rockery that needs weeding. I keep meaning to do it, but my back's not what it was." It was not a large bed, and there were two of them; it was soon done.

"I never handle money," said the wife. "You'll have to see my husband about that."

"Weeding, eh?" he said, when they presented themselves once more at the front door. "Step inside a moment, young man. Can't talk finances with a woman. Hopeless. They haven't a clue." David nodded solemnly and said, "Quite right;" Kim remained, fuming, on the doorstep. The man looked David up and down, asked if he played cricket, was told yes, and gave him a pound.

"The old rat," said Kim.

"Nobody's told him you've been liberated." David, clearly, found it very funny. Kim glared at him.

"How much did he give us anyway? Ten pence? Twenty? Does he actually know about decimal currency?"

"Two quid. Can't complain about that."

"We were worth three," Kim said. "Easily. The old rat. Oh, that reminds me — I've got a new torture to tell you."

"*How* does it remind you? Going to go back and do it to him?"

"I'd love to. It's the Rat Torture. It's terrible."

"Come on, then."

"Not now. We're working. You need to sit back and savour it."

They progressed along Addison Avenue, doing, on the whole, rather well. David had been right; the Addisonians went out of their way to be obliging. Kim and David washed cars, did two lots of shopping, tidied a toolbox and cleaned out a rabbit hutch. Kim was repeatedly told of her failure to resemble a Boy Scout. The money rolled in.

"*Over* sixteen pounds," said David.

"Really?" For four hours' work! Kim began to think the anti-mugger jacket not such a bad idea. "D'you want to stop now?"

"Just one more. Then we'll quit. I'm starving."

"Hope it's an old lady." Elderly ladies, who were a common species in Addison Avenue, had proved very susceptible to David's snub nose and cheerful, friendly grin. It was a lady, but not an old one.

"Hello!" she said, looking surprised, but smiling.

"Hello!" said David, pleased to know that he could charm the middle-aged just as well as the old, and instantaneously at that. Kim made a strangled noise. David frowned at her, and went into his speech. "We're trying to earn some extra pocket money, and we wondered if you had any jobs we could do."

"Jobs?" She hesitated, but, being an Addisonian, stopped to give the matter serious consideration, flashing the occasional amused glance at Kim, who was looking shifty. "Yes — I know. McCluskey!" This last was addressed to somebody inside the house; there was a loud thump, and a grunt, and a large shaggy Old English sheepdog shambled into the hall. "Would you take him for a walk? I'd be so very grateful. He's supposed to go twice a day. Hang on — I'll get his lead."

"Now there's a nice easy job," said David. "Just *walking*. What's the matter with you?"

"Mrs. *Hanrahan*," hissed Kim. "My *form* mistress. I never knew she lived here! How was I to know! I . . ."

"Don't get your knickers in a twist. What's wrong with that? She'll think what a nice helpful girl you are."

"But she's wearing *trousers*!" It was an unthinkable sight. Mrs. Hanrahan favoured the Sensible Skirt.

"People do," David said, amused. "Our Mr. Padmore, now, he generally wears a suit to school, but that doesn't mean he doesn't slip into a negligée the moment he gets home . . ." Mrs. Hanrahan reappeared, leading an unenthusiastic-looking McCluskey.

"He's very good," she said. "He's supposed to be trained, though trained for what I've never discovered. Half an hour will be quite enough."

Kim took the dog, and pulled experimentally on the lead, which was attached to a choke chain. "Kerry would go bananas if she saw him," she said as they set off. "She's been dying to have a dog for ages. And he is rather beautiful. Where shall we go?"

"There's a park about ten minutes from here. We could let him run. I wonder what he *is* trained to do."

They were approaching a junction; Kim stopped at the kerb and said: "Sit!" McCluskey sat. "Well! How about that! McCluskey — stand!" Nothing happened. "Stand! All right then — down!" This McCluskey was willing to do; he flopped to the ground and rested his head on his front paws. "*Good* boy. Now sit! Sit!" McCluskey feigned sleep. "Sit, you stupid dog!" But McCluskey, it seemed, had been trained in one direction only; he obeyed only those orders

53

which caused his centre of gravity to be lowered. Kim hauled him to his feet; he eyed her reproachfully.

"Let me take him for a while," said David, who was beginning to feel rather left out. Kim handed over the lead; McCluskey promptly sank to the ground again and refused to move. "Heel!" bellowed David masterfully. "Heel!" He slapped his left thigh vigorously, clicked his fingers, shouted encouragingly and slapped his thigh some more. McCluskey watched this performance with interest, but budged not an inch.

"He doesn't like you, does he?" Kim took the lead back again. "McCluskey!" The dog yawned, rose and padded to her side. *"There's* a good boy!"

"Dogs are very bad judges of character," said David, much wounded.

McCluskey liked the park. It was very much to his taste. He curled up on the grass and went to sleep. Kim and David kept an eye on him from the swings, rocking lazily to and fro. They'd had a hard morning.

"Dogs," said David, "are supposed to *gambol*. And *frisk*. But that one's much too stupid to realize it. What's that?" Another dog, a small one, was approaching, scampering purposefully over the grass. It was like a miniature McCluskey.

"A Shih Tsu, I think." Kerry could name just about any breed of dog; Kim, though less certain, had picked up a good deal of her knowledge. The Shih Tsu looked like two mops going for a walk on a set of shaggy carthorse feet. It rolled over on to its back, squirming violently and waving its legs in the air, righted itself, shook itself and went over to investigate McCluskey. McCluskey opened one eye, and prodded the Shih Tsu gently with his paw. The Shih Tsu attacked. Kim, appalled . . . "I'm sorry, Mrs. Hanrahan, but he's been savaged" . . . rushed to the rescue, managed with difficulty to detach the Shih Tsu, and grabbed a dazed-

54

looking McCluskey, who began, belatedly, to bark.

"I think we'd better go," said David, "before its owner turns up." David had very definite ideas about the type of person that owned Shih Tsus. They escaped through the nearest park gate. And there, as if waiting for them, was as welcome a sight as they could have wished for — a hot dog van. They looked at each other wordlessly; David's hand was already reaching into the anti-mugger pocket. They were ravenous.

"With onions," said Kim. "And brown sauce." She told McCluskey to sit, and waited. Opposite her stretched a broad expanse of wall, backing on to wasteland and covered with graffiti.

"Look at that," she said. David turned. Across the top of the wall was written, large, bold and white:

PROCRASTINATE NOW!

"Very good," said David, sausagefully. They crossed the road, and read on.

NEVER PUT OFF TILL TOMORROW WHAT CAN BE PUT OFF
TILL THE DAY AFTER

The theme of time was loosely continued with:

IF TIME IS RELATIVE MY AUNT ETHEL IS THE LAST
FORTNIGHT IN APRIL

then somebody digressed with:

HELP STAMP OUT CANINE DISTEMPER: STRANGLE A
SPANIEL TODAY!

which caused David to look thoughtfully at McCluskey. "Graffiti's an art form," he said to Kim as they retraced their steps to Addison Avenue. "There ought to be walls of graffiti in the National Gallery."

"The *Tate* Gallery," Kim said loftily.

Mrs. Hanrahan had a jug of iced orange waiting for them; Kim regretted the onions, which were pungent and lingered on long after their consumption.

"You didn't have any trouble with him?"

"He didn't like David at all," said Kim. "He wouldn't *move* unless I had him." It felt very strange, sitting there drinking squash inside Mrs. Hanrahan's house. Nor had Kim yet come to terms with the trousers.

"I should have thought — I could have told you that. He's the same with my son — won't do a thing for him. Adores my daughter-in-law. He's their dog, by the way. Quite likes me. Can't stand my husband."

"Men can't handle dogs," Kim said, grinning. "Hopeless. They haven't a clue. I think he's a *lovely* dog."

"He's a puzzling dog. He's very young, you know — not two years old yet. And he slouches around like an old-age pensioner. I'm sure he never *wants* to go for walks, yet apparently he *has* to be walked. We've got him for a month, while John and Rosemary are in America. He works for British Airways — they get cheap air travel. I don't suppose," she said after a moment, "either of you would like a regular job, would you? Because walking McCluskey is not, shall we say, the highlight of my day."

"I'm going away on Monday," David said. "Kim might."

"Yes, of course I would." There — she had a job. Just like that.

"Good. Mornings and evenings. All right, Kim?"

"Oh — I can't come tomorrow morning — I have to go somewhere — with my sister — but after that I can." Even on Sunday; it wouldn't be too late when she got home. "So could I start tomorrow evening?"

Mrs. Hanrahan said that she could, and went off to look for her purse.

"Isn't that good?" Kim said, as they walked home. "Didn't I do *well*?"

56

"Yes," said David. "Well done. And don't forget, you must always take your doggy kit with you."

"My what?"

"Don't you know? Dear, dear. Essential part of walking a dog, these days. I saw it on TV. You have to take a supply of little bags, some disposable gloves and a little spade. Then if there should be a mishap on a public footpath, you just slip on a glove, get out the spade, scoop the mishap into the bag and throw it away. Very hygienic."

"You're joking. With everyone watching?"

"They'll admire you, for being so public-spirited . . ." Kim grunted. Doggy kit, indeed. She could see the sense in it. But . . . well. She decided that if she saw anybody else doing it, she'd think about it. Until then she'd do the sensible thing and walk away very quickly, pretending to have nothing to do with it at all. She'd never *wanted* to be public-spirited, anyway . . .

They stopped outside the Tates' house to divide up the spoils.

"I've been counting as we went along," David said. "Eighteen pounds."

"But that's fantastic." Kim had started out with thoughts of a fiver if she was lucky. They must have more money than they knew what to do with. "Eighteen quid . . . is that before or after the hot dogs?"

"Oh, after," David said vaguely, and counted out nine pounds for Kim. The rest of the money, most of which had been given to him by his mother when he went in to fetch his jacket, he put back. Their actual takings had been ten pounds fifty; he'd decided to keep one pound fifty for himself, for not even David was generous enough, or foolish enough, to do a whole morning's work for nothing at all.

5

"IF I WERE YOU, KIM, I'd bring a book along. There's likely to be a fair bit of waiting around." Mrs. Tate was a veteran of these outings; Kim nodded gloomily and reached for the detective story she'd brought from the library, but there was only one chapter left, and she'd guessed who the murderer was anyhow, back in chapter ten. That wouldn't do. Then she remembered *Pride and Prejudice*, their set book for next term; Mr. Coles had given out the copies already on the offchance that *some* of 2K might be far-sighted enough to get it read, or at least *begun*, during the holidays. In the atmosphere of end-of-term euphoria this had seemed most unlikely. But now — it was just the book for the occasion. Endless, and tiresome. She dug it out of her schoolbag, a miserable and ancient-looking volume, bearing the inevitable label listing its former owners. Judging by the condition of the book, each one of them had thrown it repeatedly against the wall. Kim glanced at the pages, and winced. Such small print. And so much of it.

Kerry was ready. She had been placed in the middle of the settee, out of harm's way, for Kerry was always especially clumsy on psychologist mornings. One saucer had hit the deck already.

"Right — on your feet, you two. The bus goes in *eight*

and a half minutes . . ." Kim grabbed Kerry and steered her safely through the front door; Mrs. Tate followed, issuing last-minute reminders to Frances over her shoulder.

"Gone!" said Anna darkly, as the door slammed. Anna found psychologists, and her sister's continual visits to them, very dreary. Just because Anna went to school every day without fussing, she was taken for granted. Nobody thought to ask *her* if she liked it. Nobody gave *her* tests — and Anna would have done so well at the tests! — and if it wasn't that she enjoyed school so much *she* wouldn't go either, and that would show them.

"Isn't it quiet," said Frances. They were finishing their breakfast in a leisurely fashion; it was pleasant to watch other people tearing around hurrying to catch a bus. Anna remedied the quietness by switching on the radio.

"Mum's last day at work," Frances said. "Well, half day, really." Mrs. Tate was going straight from the psychologist to take her final bow at Wilshires; Kim would bring Kerry home. Anna thought it would be marvellous, having her mother at home all day. It was quite horrible of Kim to go around saying stern things about Cutting Back, and Tightening of Belts. Anna did not intend her own belt to be tightened one iota of a notch. Kim had gone out yesterday and come back with some money, and saying that she'd got a job, and instead of telling her not to be so silly, that they had *plenty* of money, Mrs. Tate had been very pleased with her. The important fact that emerged from all this was that it now looked less likely than ever that Anna would be allowed to go to the Josephine Priestley School.

They sat in a companionable sort of silence, Anna listening to Bill Maloney's Kidsline and brooding on her own misfortunes, Frances reading the newspaper. They had always got on well together; four years was a convenient gap, and their tastes were not dissimilar, nor were they unlike in looks, so far as was possible in a family like the Tates, none of whom strongly resembled any of the others. Frances was fond of Anna; Anna found Frances a haven of sympathy in a world that seemed so often determined to thwart her in every way.

Frances wasn't exactly *reading* the newspaper. She *meant* to, but somehow it wasn't happening. It was all to do with her move from primary to secondary school; she kept feeling that she really must start to do things like — well, like reading the papers. But most of it was so very dull. Foreign affairs, the economy, the energy crisis, the car workers' strike . . . There were always the crosswords, but Frances wasn't very good at crosswords, not even the straightforward ones. Her father had spent hours on end sitting over crosswords — weird ones with no black squares and great long rambling senseless clues that boggled Frances's brain. She thought them a terrible waste of time. So she looked at the fashion page, the television pages and the cartoons. Nobody could deny that she was reading the newspaper. She just wasn't reading the news.

Anna was looking doleful. "Don't you like this?" Frances asked kindly, meaning Kidsline.

"Not much." It was too much talk; Anna liked records. "Frances?"

"Mmm?"

"I'm not going to go to the Josephine Priestley School. Am I."

Frances folded the paper back on itself and laid it on the table. "No, Anna. Really you're not."

"I don't think it's right. Do you? That people should be let to go there because of the money they've got and not because they're . . ."

"Talented. No, it doesn't seem right. I suppose they do give some scholarships . . ."

"What's that?"

"Well" — oh dear — "it means that sometimes they take

60

pupils without their parents paying the whole of the fees."

"Then I could . . ."

"But we could never afford even *part* of the fees, even if you *won* a scholarship. Really we couldn't. Not unless we won on a Premium Bond or something."

Anna apparently accepted this, but Frances could see the word 'scholarship' being carefully filed away in her brain.

"Anyway, Anna, I bet if you *were* at stage school and you *had* to do all that dancing and acting and stuff it would just be like hard work. Not fun. And it's probably only a very few children who get into the ads and TV serials and things. There's never enough of that sort of thing to go round all the people who want to do it. Imagine how awful it would be, watching other children go off and make ads while you had to stay behind. *Much* worse than watching them on television."

There was no possibility that she would have been one of the rejected stay-behinds. Had she been with Kim Anna would have said this. But this was Frances; she sighed, and said: "Oh, *Frances*," and flopped forlornly forward on to the table, eyes peeking over her arm.

"Aren't you going to finish your Rice Krispies?"

"They're all dead by now." This meant that they had ceased to snap, to crackle, to pop. Anna thought dead Rice Krispies very nasty indeed. All soggy and horr . . . "Frances! Look at this! What is it? Let me see!"

"See what?" Frances asked, bemused, as the paper was snatched from her hand. And then she caught sight of the words 'Dairy Princess' . . . Anna was scanning the page rapidly.

"Listen while I read you what it says! 'The hunt is on for the Dairy Princess of Great Britain . . . between the ages of six and ten . . . regional heats and a national Grand Final in September . . . contestants will be judged on appearance and personality . . . ' "

"Do you get anything if you win?"

"I'm *telling* you! 'The winner will receive a prize of two hundred and fifty pounds . . . will be Dairy Princess for a year . . . her picture will be used in publicity for your Daily Pinta' . . . and I'll ride on the Milk Float in next year's Grand Carnival attended by six Milkmaids of Honour . . ." On a glittering throne! Sipping cool fresh milk through two straws . . . in a creamy white robe . . . an icy Snow Queen, a beautiful summer pinta glorious Dairy Princess! It was too wonderful to be true! She remembered, suddenly, what she had heard somebody say on television the other day — God never closes one door without opening another. God was on her side! How could she lose? She looked so lovely all in white . . .

"Anna, you haven't won it yet." Frances hadn't missed the change from third person to first.

"Not yet . . .'To get your entry form just buy a carton of double cream from your milkman . . . ' " Oh! She couldn't wait till the milkman came tomorrow morning! She would die!

"Well, that's all right. It's his pay day. He's always much later on Fridays."

"You mean he hasn't been yet?"

"That's right. Didn't you hear Mum saying she'd leave the milk money on the hall table?"

"I didn't notice. Oh, Frances!"

"Yes, I know. Cool *down*. Dairy Princesses have to be cool. I don't know what Mum's going to say, though," she added after a moment. "Beauty contests. You've heard what she says about them. She *hates* them."

"Yes, but that's different! That's ladies wobbling up and down in swimming costumes! This is a *Dairy Princess*."

"I suppose it isn't really the same, no." Milk was so very respectable. Squeaky-clean and healthy. "Oh, Lord, here *is* the milkman. No, you stay there."

"A carton of double cream," said Anna, and beamed happily at her unfinished bowl of cereal, which suddenly seemed quite different, for the dead Rice Krispies were floating in beautiful, delicious milk. It was her favourite drink of all. Anna was only now realizing this.

"Going to be Dairy Princess, are you?" asked the milkman.

"Not *me*! I'm too old, anyway. It's for my little sister."

"If she's half as pretty as you," the milkman said gallantly, "she'll romp home." He blinked; an apparition had materialized in the front window. A small girl, clutching a tall glass of milk with a couple of straws in it . . . she waggled her fingers at him. "Er, yes," said the milkman, and waved back, sheepishly, for which he was rewarded with a flash of milky-white teeth. Frances, able to see only the milkman's side of this, was puzzled.

The milkman pulled himself together. "Er — you're thirty-four pence short, love."

"What? But she always leaves enough . . . oh, the cream."

"Shall I add it on to next week's?"

"No — better not — hang on a moment." Frances disappeared indoors. The milkman squinted at the window. The girl was still there, only now, in addition to the glass, she was holding a *pint* of milk in the other hand. He wondered if there was some deep significance to all this which was eluding him. Frances returned, and paid him. "Good luck, then," said the milkman, and fled without looking back. The girl might by now have produced a Jersey cow; he didn't think he could bear that.

Anna grabbed the entry form. "Let's fill it in *straight away*. We could catch the midday post . . ."

"It's not a *race*, Anna . . . Why have you got a pint of milk in your hand? . . . Shall I fill it in for you?"

Anna thought of her own writing, which was very *good*,

but perhaps a little on the big side for filling in forms. She agreed that Frances should.

"There isn't much to put, actually." Frances began to write. "Name — address — date of birth — oh, and there's a space that says 'signature of parent or guardian', so we can't post it yet."

"Oh." Anna began to panic. "When's the closing date? When . . ."

"August the fourth. *Plenty* of time. Listen to this. You'll be in the London and South-east heat, on August the twenty-third. They'll send full details when they receive your entry."

"What else does it say? What's all that on the back?"

"It's just — Anna, stop bouncing, you're making me seasick — it's only repeating what was in the paper. The age limit — you're all right there — and about the publicity and the carnival. That's *all*. See for yourself."

"What shall I wear? I'll have to have a new dress."

"You've got plenty of dresses!"

"But not a white one . . . and everyone will be wearing a new dress! I must have one. I know. I'll ask Dad to let me have my birthday present early."

"Two *months* early?"

"Oh, he won't mind." In fact, by the time her birthday arrived he would probably have forgotten, and would buy her another present as well. Anna's birthday fell just three days after Kerry's, which always struck her as terribly unfair. Everybody had already used up all their birthdayness on Kerry. And then she remembered that by the time her birthday arrived she would be the Dairy Princess, and it would be a national event. She imagined all the milkmen in the country going to work with a song in their hearts and a smile on their faces, because Anna Tate, their Princess, was eight . . . the phrase 'Eight Glorious Years' went through her mind . . . perhaps the farmers could tie yellow ribbons on to the tails of all the dairy cows . . .

"The money would be useful," said Frances. "Even if you came third, you'd get seventy-five pounds."

Anna wasn't interested in third. Two hundred and fifty pounds . . . until that moment she had been thinking only about the glory and the fame. Now she thought about the money, and Frances had no difficulty at all in picking up the direction of her thoughts.

"It wouldn't be enough to pay the fees, Anna. Not nearly enough; not even if you *won*. So don't think about it."

Anna smiled. *Reduced* fees, she thought. Scholarship. God had left *both* doors open.

Kim had been sitting in the waiting room for fifty-five minutes: the first ten with her mother and Kerry, and now three-quarters of an hour on her own. There was a receptionist sort of person behind a desk in the far corner, and during the last ten minutes Kim had been joined by three other waiters: a woman with a small boy, and a short, stout black lady who had emerged from one of the rooms down the corridor, where her child, presumably, was still grappling with an Expert. These two women had fallen into conversation. Kim had managed to get through twenty pages of *Pride and Prejudice*, but it was very difficult to concentrate; she was wondering if Kerry was getting upset, and brooding about her own interview which was to follow shortly. She kept reading the same paragraph again and again, but the words refused to fit together into any sort of meaning. So she gave up, and listened to the women.

The white one was doing most of the talking, occasionally jerking her son's elbow or tapping his head to emphasize a point. "I don't think they know what they're doing here any more. Six months ago we thought Duane" — tap — "was coming along nicely. He was seeing Mrs. Lucas then. Did you know Mrs. Lucas?" The black woman shook her head.

"Well, she's gone now. Just when he was getting to trust her, weren't you, Duane?" — jerk — "He stopped attacking people altogether. We were *hopeful*. But now — all pretty talk. And drawing pictures! I won't have that. Not after the last time. Have they tried that on your lad yet? Drawing pictures?"

"My Michael don't draw pictures for nobody," the black woman said gloomily. "He tell them what they can do with their pictures. Oh brother."

"I'll tell you what they did with Duane" — tap — "last time we came. They gave him a piece of paper and some crayons, and asked him would he like to draw a nice picture while they talked to Mummy. And he thought he was just drawing something to take home with him! As soon as he'd drawn something they snatched it away from him — didn't they, Duane?" — jerk — "and looked at it and whispered together and told me it *meant* things. He'd drawn a woman, you see, so they said: 'Is that Mummy, Duane?' and he told them it was and they decided he had a mother-fixation. And on the way home he said to me: 'Mum, I was going to draw Dad as well, and Sharon and Gary and Kevin and Melody and me, all in a row. They didn't give me time to finish it!' So that just shows you."

Kim was appalled. It was a most underhand thing to do. It was spying on someone's mind: bugging their brain. A voice, down the corridor, began to shout abuse. "That Michael," said the black woman. The white one listened, and froze. She grabbed Duane, who was looking interested, and put her hands over his ears. The shouts died away, but not before Kim had considerably broadened her vocabulary.

Out came Mr. Gilbert, with Mrs. Tate and Kerry, who was holding an ominous piece of paper and a pencil.

"Hel*lo*," said Mr. Gilbert. "You must be Kim. Now, I'm just going to have a little word with Mummy, and then you can come in and we'll have a little chat. And Kerry's going to draw a picture, aren't you, Kerry?" Kerry smiled, but not very much. The receptionist called: "Mrs. Wilkinson!" and the white woman departed down the corridor, propelling Duane in front of her. "Yak yak *yak*," said the black one. Kim flashed her a sympathetic grin, and turned to Kerry.

"Do you *want* to draw a picture?"

"Not really." Kerry appeared to have come through relatively unscathed; she looked suspicious, but not unduly disturbed.

"Did you tell *him* you did?"

"No." She thought about it. "He told *me* I did."

"But you don't. D'you fancy a game of noughts and crosses?"

"Oh yes — all right."

"Good." Kim took the pencil and rapidly drew a series of large noughts and crosses grids all over the paper — both sides of it. "We'll have to take turns with the pencil. Right — you go first."

"You're not to let me win," said Kerry, who never minded losing, but always knew when somebody was allowing her to win, and hated that. She drew a cross in the centre of the first grid.

Some ten minutes later Mrs. Tate came out, and sent Kim in. "Noughts and crosses?" she said.

"Kerry felt like a game. It's so boring for her, sitting around here."

"Did you, darling? Shall I take over? I don't think he's going to keep you very long, Kim. Now, Kerry. Who's winning?"

"We keep drawing," Kerry said. "We're too good for each other."

For some reason Kim had pictured Mr. Gilbert as either very old or very young, but he was neither; he was distinctly middle-aged, with gold-rimmed glasses and a face that was not a success. His dark hair was receding, as if straining to get away from the face. His clothes were casual; his voice softly encouraging.

"Now, if we could just go over a few things, Kim. I'd like you to tell me, in your own words, when you first began to notice that Kerry was unhappy about school."

"Well. It was towards the end of the first year. I was still there, then. It didn't get really bad until the second year, though."

"Do you think your moving to secondary school might have had anything to do with it?"

"No. I told you. It started when I was still at primary school."

"As I see it, she lost two of the people closest to her, within a very short time. In different ways. You went off to a different school, and Daddy went away altogether. How did Kerry seem to feel about that? Was she very distressed?"

"Not really. It didn't affect her so much."

"Her *Daddy* going *away*? She didn't *mind*? That doesn't seem quite natural, does it?"

"I didn't say she didn't *mind* my father going away. She just didn't go bananas about it, that's all. She was very young. And it can't have had anything to do with the school thing, because that had already begun. I told you that."

"Did you mind when he went away?"

What could you say? 'No' wasn't natural, and 'yes' — God knows what he'd make of a 'yes' — and she couldn't keep silent because that would sound like she meant 'yes' but it was too painful to talk about . . . "I was very young, too," she said defensively.

"You were twelve, Kim."

"Yes, that's right." Every time she spoke he nodded, as if her words had been in some way deeply significant.

"How do you think Mummy felt about it?"

"You'd have to ask her that." *None of your business! And what's that got to do with Kerry?* Oh, God. This was even worse than she'd expected. How was it possible to be polite and helpful when all her instincts were to hate him? How could her mother *bear* it when they asked her these questions? Kim's insides were twisting up with the effort of it.

Mr. Gilbert smiled, wisely, knowingly. "I see." He opened a file and glanced briefly at a piece of paper. *What did it say?* Had he got private things written down about her mother and father? She wanted to snatch it out of his hands. She wanted to hit him.

"Kim, I'd like to talk about Anna."

"Huh? Oh, all right. What about her?"

"She's a very bright little girl, is that right? And attractive. I'm trying, you see, to understand how you, in your family, get along together."

"We get along fine."

"Do you think Kerry might be jealous of Anna? That she might find it a little difficult to compete with her? Anna is the youngest, after all — perhaps a little spoiled? — it's really quite likely."

"Kerry jealous of *Anna*? No way. Kerry was never in her life jealous of anybody. The other way round, if anything."

"Anna jealous of Kerry, you mean? Now why should that be? Perhaps because Kerry gets so much attention, through not going to school?"

"Something like that."

"Do you think Kerry might be doing it to get attention?"

"*No*." You couldn't win. She shouldn't have said anything. "She's not *like* that. She's not 'doing' anything. It's not the way to put it."

"How would you put it?"

"School's done it to her."

"I *see*. You feel that the trouble definitely lies with the school."

"Not *with* it. At it." Surely that was obvious.

69

"Well, all right, let's explore that. I wonder how she got along with the other children. She doesn't seem to be much of a mixer."

"She gets on O.K. with the other kids. She's got a few friends living near us. But she actually prefers to be on her own a lot of the time. She can always amuse herself, you know. But she plays with Anna, because Anna *can't* amuse herself, not very well."

"Do you think she might have been bullied?"

"No. It's impossible that anyone could have been bullying Kerry without me knowing. It's nothing like that; nothing to do with *people*. I know it isn't."

Mr. Gilbert cleared his throat. "Kim — when I was talking to Kerry I found myself wondering if she was really very stupid, or really very clever."

"You wouldn't say that to me if you thought she was stupid. So you must think she's clever." This took the wind out of his sails; it had spoiled his next sentence, she could see.

"Yes. I do. And I gave her some puzzles to solve. Quite simple things, with blocks and shapes. A bright child of eight should solve any of them in less than half a minute. Kerry took a minute and a half, sometimes longer. And I got the impression she wasn't trying. Now why should that be?"

"Well — Kerry's like that. You can't hurry her."

"I wasn't hurrying her. *She* didn't know how long they should have taken."

"I don't know then. Perhaps she wasn't trying. She isn't very — what's the word? — competitive."

"All the same. I can't think why a bright child should be so anxious to *hide* her intelligence. To disguise it. Unless she's playing a rather clever game with us — trying to convince us that she's too backward to be sent to school."

"I honestly don't think she's that devious." What

rubbish. The conversation was just going round in circles. Mr. Gilbert would suggest something, and Kim would say no, that doesn't sound like Kerry at all. It seemed very pointless. But at least now they were discussing *Kerry*, and she liked that better than she had the early part of the interview. Not a lot, but better. And she had been very glad to hear that he had acknowledged Kerry's intelligence without question — even if he did think she was using it to play tricks on him.

"We don't seem to be getting very far, do we?"

"Not really."

"You don't much like answering my questions, do you?"

"No. Not really." There seemed little point in pretending; Kim knew she had never been any good at hiding her feelings.

"We'd better leave it at that, then," he said abruptly. "I had hoped you might try to be more helpful, for your sister's sake. However." Kim had a sinking sensation of having let everybody down — which was doubtless what he meant her to feel — but she couldn't help it. She'd done her best; she hadn't lost her temper, and she didn't *think* she'd been rude. Well — not very. "Let's go and see what Kerry's been drawing."

"She was drawing lots of crosses when I left her."

"*Nothing* but crosses?"

"Nothing." Mr. Gilbert frowned at this, as if pondering for the first time the possibility that Kerry's problem might be religious mania.

He frowned even more when he saw Mrs. Tate and Kerry, still playing away happily.

"Noughts and crosses? What's this? I thought Kerry was going to draw a picture!"

"Well, she's never really much liked drawing," said her mother. "And she's been enjoying this. These visits are always something of an ordeal for her."

Mr. Gilbert was looking very displeased indeed. "This is really . . . well . . ." At this point Kerry crossed her legs, wriggled and said urgently: "Mum, I've got to *go*" and, with that, the Tates made their departure.

They decided to go to McDonalds for burgers and chips. On the way, Kim related the gist of her interview; her mother seemed neither surprised nor displeased.

"You didn't actually tell him to mind his own business?"

"Not once."

"Well, that's just about as much as I hoped for. I never expected that you'd be the slightest help to him, but he would insist. Shall I tell you his theory?" Kerry had scampered on ahead to save a table; Kim nodded. "He reckons that since her father went away Kerry's got a morbid fear that everyone's going to desert her. She's afraid that if she's at school all day everyone else — particularly me — may disappear while she's gone."

"But that's so stupid! It's *obviously* stupid. For one thing, you aren't in the house where she can keep an eye on you, you're out at work. And she doesn't stay at home anyway, she goes to Gran's. And it's only *school*. She doesn't mind going anywhere else."

"Yes, I know all that. If her father had gone while she was actually at school, I might think perhaps there was something in it. But it was during the Christmas holidays."

"Do you honestly believe this Mr. Gilbert is going to solve anything, Mum?"

"Oh, I don't know. Half of me *always* expects that they're on the verge of finding the answer. The other half thinks *we're* on the verge of finding it. I suppose you'd call that the optimist's version of hedging your bets."

"I was a lot more optimistic *before* I met him."

"So was I . . . still, as he said, it's the first time he's seen her. They haven't had a chance to build up a relationship yet. And he didn't upset her — he wasn't at all threatening.

It's dangerous to rely too much on first impressions," she added. Kim shrugged; if Kerry built up any sort of a relationship with him ever, she'd be very surprised. And it sounded as if it was going to take ages after all — no instant magical solution, and September was only five weeks away . . . but she wasn't going to be disheartening, so she switched the conversation to the puzzles, and the possibility that Kerry was for some reason trying to appear far stupider than she actually was. Mrs. Tate nodded with interest; Kerry was *always* like that with puzzles and tests. You could see that she wasn't making any effort at all. "You know," she said, quite excitedly, "I'd never thought about it in that way before. I always assumed that she just had an aversion to tests because they were like school; in her mind, at least. Let's try and figure it out, Kim. I've got an idea that this might be the key to the whole thing."

They turned in to McDonalds; Kim went up to get the food. It didn't take long; they were ahead of the lunchtime rush, and there were more people serving than there were customers. "Less than a minute," Mrs. Tate said with admiration, helping Kim unload the tray. "Absolutely marvellous. When I used to go out to lunch with my parents all we did was wait. Wait for the waitress to take our order. Wait for her to bring it. Repeat that for every course. Catch her eye. Wait for her to give us our bill. Wait for her to come back so we could pay it. I used to die of impatience. This is so much better."

"Old ladies like you," Kim said cruelly, "aren't supposed to approve of Fast Food."

"*Cheeky*," said her mother, and swiped four of her chips. "Hey, I'll be getting my present today. They've been in such a frantic rush, trying to make a collection, and at the end of the week at that. It's been so funny to watch."

"What do you think you'll have?" Kerry asked.

"More than likely a radio alarm. That's the thing at the

"That's just it. He hasn't got one. He's bragging just the way we did when we didn't have one."

"Well, what do you know," Wilbur said.

"Gosh sakes," Bunky said.

The three of them grinned at one another, and then they continued up Plum Street looking for prospective members for the Plum Street Athletic Club. Especially a certain one with big hands.

"*There* you are," said a voice from next door. It was not addressed to Anna, but she sat to attention all the same, and, suddenly much more cheerful, resumed her gorgeous glow. It was David Holder. He'd just climbed up on to next door's garage roof, from where he could see Anna very well, and David liked Anna, she knew it — he called her Goldilocks, and sometimes more doubtful things like Fragrant Fruit-drop, which caused Anna's eldest sister Kim to splutter with mirth. But blow Kim. Anna had her audience. She glowed.

"Silly little noodle," Kim said to David, across the three-foot gap between their respective roofs.

"She's only seven," David said, tolerantly.

Kim began to say: "Nearly eight, and if she lives to see nine it'll be a miracle" — but she couldn't be bothered to argue. It was too hot. "I wonder if this'll last for the whole six weeks," she said instead.

"I expect it'll manage to rain for August Bank Holiday. And all through next week while we're away."

"Where did you say you were going?"

"Scotland. Eleven days, actually."

"Oh aye. I remember. Well, be sure to comb your sporran every day — and eat up your porridge — and bring us back some Edinburgh rock."

"We aren't going to Edinburgh. We're going to the Highlands. I'll be able to do some climbing. I might bring you back a haggis."

"*Thanks* — oh, I know. Tie a label round Bryony's neck saying 'Caber'. And perhaps somebody'll toss her."

"Lovely thought," David said wistfully, "but she's not coming. Didn't you know? We're going to stay with our frightfully best friend Camilla. They've got a *dinky* little pad in the country. Two up two down. And that's just the bathrooms."

Kim nodded, unsurprised. Bryony and David both went

report. How did that get there? It hasn't even been opened."

Frances looked, not without apprehension, at the thin brown envelope. "I'll have one of those at Christmas."

"Mmm, I can't imagine you at Thornton Park, you know. I'm too used to you being at Priory Lane."

"Why?" Frances couldn't imagine herself there, come to that.

"Don't know. Just can't. Well — can you imagine Anna where you are now? In the top form?"

"No," said Frances. "And it's where I *was*. I'm not there any more. Kim — do you really not know if Janice and I'll be put in the same form? Haven't you *any* idea?"

"Not a clue. I've told you. In the second year you're put into streams according to how you did in the first year exams. But nobody knows how they decide who goes where in the first year. It seems like absolutely pot luck. Perhaps they draw names out of a hat."

"Oh well." Frances took Kim's report and peered at the envelope, as if the answer to her problem might be found within. "You know, I don't think Mum would notice if you never gave her this. She's not interested in reports at all."

"Oh, one of those things," said Mrs. Tate, when presented with the envelope. "Where did you find it, darling?"

"Down a crack in the armchair."

"You've done a wonderful job on that room. I think you should be . . ."

"Aren't you going to open it?" asked Anna, who *was* interested in Kim's report, and didn't want the subject changed.

"Oh, reports," said Mrs. Tate. "Kim, are you doing as well as you can at school?"

"Yes."

"Have you been in any serious trouble or disgraced the family name?"

"Certainly not."

moment, radio alarms. Everyone's getting them. It could be worse. It used to be vases. Even Betty Mitchell — she was allergic to flowers, couldn't have them in her house, but they gave her vases just the same."

"I wonder what they'll give Mr. Wilshire when he retires." A little coffin, thought Kim, with his initials on the side . . .

"Mr. Wilshire," said her mother, "will never retire. Never. They'll have to wheel him out in a coffin." Kim choked. "And even then he'll still run the store. Instead of staff meetings they'll hold weekly seances, and Mr. Wilshire will issue his orders from the Other Side. He'll organize Heaven into departments in no time . . . tell Saint Peter to have a more attractive display at the entrance to bring in the customers." They laughed; soon the psychologist was quite forgotten.

6

UNLIKE HIS MOTHER, Mr. Tate never mentioned the fact that he had a favourite, but everybody knew it just the same. There had always been a special, indefinable sort of bond between him and his eldest daughter. Kim adored her father. She was fascinated by his mind, which seemed to her to soar up into the stratosphere, making more ordinary thought processes like her own seem earthy and leaden by comparison. There was nobody like him. It was not surprising that in the Tate household he had often seemed isolated by his own genius. And she loved so many other things about him: his kindness, his gentleness, the way he never shouted or lost his temper as their mother did; his placid serenity, his dreaminess, his patient way of explaining things to a dense daughter. Of course he had faults. He was absent-minded and forgetful; he was easily bored, and at times seemed to withdraw into himself completely. But these were very trivial; Kim longed to be like him, and knew she never would. She was too much like her mother. And you *couldn't* be like both of them — they were poles apart.

She looked around hopefully as she jumped off the bus, with a book under one arm and a bag of bananas under the other. He nearly always came to meet her in the car; but not, apparently, today. Oh well. It was fifteen minutes' walk.

But perhaps he would meet her half-way.

It was good to be spending an afternoon in the quiet peace of her father's flat. There had been the almightiest row at home on Friday evening, and the reverberations had not yet ceased. Kim had foreseen the whole thing, the moment she heard about the Dairy Princess contest. Nobody could say she hadn't warned them. But Anna, wildly excited, took not the slightest notice; the moment Mrs. Tate came home, bearing her radio alarm clock and finished with Wilshires for ever, she thrust the entry form at her, and a pen, and demanded that she sign it *now*, this *minute* . . . Mrs. Tate took one look at it and threw it into the bin. Anna knew quite well, she said, what she thought of beauty contests — and to hold them for children was *especially* detestable. If Anna was misguided enough to enter one when she grew up, that was Anna's problem. And Frances should have known better. What had she been thinking of?

The scene that followed had been unforgettable. Anna had not screamed so loudly since she was a small baby, and her lungs, always magnificent, had gained in power since then. She shrieked to the world that she *hated* her mother; she was horrible, and mean, and she wished she was *dead*. She wished everybody was dead! This much her mother tolerated, but then Anna, a tiny blonde fury, seized the teapot and hurled it against the wall. She was promptly dragged, screaming and kicking, to bed. Immediately, she began to cry. Anna very seldom cried, but when she did it was loud and long. She could howl for two hours with no trouble at all. Mrs. Tate, provoked beyond reason, took it out on Frances — a carton of double cream? Did Frances know what that cost? She was a stupid, unthinking little idiot . . . Frances, already racked with remorse and guilt, promptly started to cry herself. They all went to bed early, in the end. Nobody slept.

The next day Mrs. Tate apologized profusely to Frances.

She hadn't meant it; Frances was a marvellous girl, she couldn't do without her. Frances apologized to her mother. Anna, silent and glowering, made it quite clear that *she* was forgiving *nobody*, not ever. She packed a bag and walked out. She would run away; she would never go back, and they would be sorry. But after wandering around for an hour or so she grew very bored, and went to her grandmother's. She would go home very late indeed, and they would all be frantic. But they weren't frantic — Mrs. Tate (who had rung her mother-in-law shortly after Anna's departure to say that Anna would probably be coming round, and would she keep her there for the day please?) just said: "Oh, there you are. Your tea's under the grill, if you want it." They didn't care! She could have been murdered! She wished she *had* been murdered . . .

So home was not, at present, the most pleasant place to be. Kim turned the corner into her father's road: a long straight road lined by tall houses, the type that had once had servants' quarters beneath and children above, and were now all converted to flats. Kim thought it vastly amusing that the basement flat of her father's house should be occupied by a man called Butler, while the couple living in the top flat were called Young. Her father lived on the second floor; she let herself in through the front door, which was ajar, and began to climb.

"Kim!" her father kissed her on the cheek. "No, I *hadn't* forgotten you were coming. I've got some cakes in specially." He was a very long, thin, ungainly-looking man; his arms and legs sprawled awkwardly around in all sorts of improbable directions. There always seemed to be more of them than he could control. His face was craggily plain: a captivating face, full of humour and wisdom. "What are you reading?" He looked at the cover of her book. "*The Mystery of the Second Ostrich*. I don't know, Kim. You've got the most appalling taste."

"Yes, I know," Kim agreed happily. "Ah, but d'you know what else I'm reading? *Pride and Prejudice*."

"Really? For school, no doubt . . . What do you think of it?"

"It's not as bad as I was expecting, actually. I like the woman — the mother. She's great."

"Mrs. *Bennet*? You like her? But she's the most awful creature."

"Yes — that's what's so good. She reminds me of Hilda Ogden in *Coronation Street*. Have you been eating properly?" He looked thinner than ever. She went into the kitchen — a tiny little room, it was — and investigated the cupboards. There was practically nothing in them; the cooker showed few signs of use. "You haven't, have you? You can't be *trusted*."

"Of course I've been eating. If I hadn't I'd be dead."

Kim sniffed. "I've brought you a bunch of bananas."

"Have you?" Her father untwisted the paper bag, and broke off a banana. "You're a sweet girl. I'll have one straight away."

"There, you see! You're hungry."

"I'm sorry Frances couldn't come," Mr. Tate said, deftly changing the subject. "It's so long since I saw her."

"Oh, well, she'd already arranged, you see, to do something else, and it would have been very awkward to cancel it." Not very convincing, but the best she could do. The truth was that Frances had announced point blank that she didn't *want* to come, and could not be persuaded to change her mind. But of course Kim couldn't tell him that; he would have been so hurt.

"How are you all?"

"Oh, we're fine." Mrs. Tate had said she wasn't to tell him about losing the job; it would accomplish nothing, there was no point. "Kerry's started seeing another psychologist. I went too."

"Oh, yes, I know about that — your mother phoned. What did you think of him?"

"I try not to think of him at all," Kim said, and they laughed. Mr. Tate peeled another banana. "Anna's in a bit of a — a mood just now, but she'll get over it. Kerry's O.K. — shooting up like mad. She's growing out of all her clothes; I think she'll be tall like me. Oh, and I've got a job. Walking a dog. To earn some extra pocket money."

"Oh, that's good. You're all right for money, are you? Should I send some more?"

"Well, actually, Dad, I think you've been forgetting. Mum said you haven't sent any at all, for a long time."

"Oh, no! Oh, I am sorry, Kim. Is my name terribly mud?"

"Not mud at all. But your memory's going to pot. Couldn't you write reminders on a calendar or something?"

"I haven't got a calendar," said her father, "and if I bought one I'd probably forget to look at it. There's no hope for me at all. Well, I'll write a cheque this minute, and you can take it back with you. I've got quite a bit of money at the moment. I'll make it out for two hundred pounds."

"Two *hundred*? Can you spare all that? Don't leave yourself short."

"I won't be short. I don't need much. Actually — I thought you'd have noticed that it wasn't outside — I've sold the car."

"You've what? But — Dad! It was only a couple of years old! Why?"

"It wasn't getting much use, you know. I was only driving to work and back, except when I came over to you." It had been agreed that Mr. Tate should take the car; he was not nearly so well served by public transport. "Petrol, road tax, insurance, repairs — with all those running costs it just wasn't worth keeping it."

This sounded sensible . . . though he might have asked

them if *they* wanted it . . ."But how are you going to get to work, now? Walk all the way to the bus?"

"Well — I'm not working, just at the moment. The money I got for the car — it's more than I'd have earned in months. And I'll have that much more time to work on the book. It seemed a good idea all round."

"Oh. Do you really think the car money will last till the book's finished, then?"

"Difficult to say, exactly. But it should last a fair while. This isn't a very expensive lifestyle."

"No. You're *not eating*."

Her father pulled a face at her, and picked up his banana skins. "I'll go and make some tea. I'm a rotten host, I know."

"No you're not. Shall I do it?"

"No, no, you sit there. By the way — I wouldn't say anything to your mother just yet. About the car. I'll tell her myself when the time seems right. O.K.?"

"O.K." All these things both her parents kept asking her not to tell the other. It was a nuisance; you had to watch your words so carefully, or things just seemed to blurt themselves out when you weren't looking. Kim was a prime blurter. It was a pity about the car — she'd liked it. He'd be awfully cut off, now. And at the end of it — here Kim suddenly saw the catch — the Tates would be left without a car, and without the means to buy another. It hadn't sounded like that when her father was explaining; he'd made it sound as if in the long run there would be no difference at all. Oh *well* — at least he was spending more time writing now. He understood the urgency.

She wandered over to the writing table in the corner. The sacred shrine. Books, books, books . . . there were more of them here every time she came. "Do you really read *all* of these?" she called.

"Not *all* of *all* of them. They're for reference. I pick out the relevant bits."

"How many have you got here?"

"Around fifty. The library have been marvellous, tracking down obscure titles for me — and I have them out on extended loan, so I needn't worry about renewals." There were books on the table, books in piles on the floor, some with markers in, some with scribbled notes poking out. It was all very impressive. All around the room was evidence of her father's cerebral pursuits: rows of crossword books, magazines folded back at the crossword page, books of mathematical brain-teasers, a chess-board with pieces set out and books of chess problems. This was his idea of relaxation.

Every one of the library books, though, was about Russia. Twentieth-century Russia. Russian customs and habits, Russians at work and at play, Communism, the Orthodox Church, Lenin and Stalin and Khrushchev, the Russian system of education, sport, the Russian economy, geography and climate. For the book he was writing was a sweeping Russian family saga, spanning the years from the turn of the century, when there had still been a Tsar, through revolution, two world wars and the Stalin years, to the late nineteen fifties and the dawning of the space age. Never had there been such a novel. Kim had looked in bookshops, especially amongst best-selling paperbacks, and had seen that her father was quite right. Sweeping family sagas did very nicely indeed. The trouble was that they took so very long to write — and Mr. Tate had never actually *been* to Russia, so he had no helpful first-hand knowledge or personal impressions to fall back on. The Russians wouldn't have allowed him to go around asking questions anyhow. It was a massive thing to take on: a very ambitious project. How many people would think of it, let alone *do* it?

The book was built around two central characters, a brother and sister called Vladimir and Irina; their lives were

81

inextricably intertwined. This much Kim knew; also that Vladimir was well-meaning but weak — he fell to pieces whenever tragedy or danger came his way, which was often, and Irina, who sounded a right little toughie, picked him up and put him back together again. Mr. Tate had told her that real characters and events would be woven into the text; this required a tremendous amount of research, but it would make the book much more realistic and believable.

Well, he'd done a fair bit of weaving, judging by the pile of manuscript. It was always kept in the same place: in a buff cardboard file at the back of the table. Kim had a good look. It was an awful mess. But it was a book, or growing into a book. "How much of this would you say you'd done?" she asked casually, as her father came back with mugs of tea and a plate of cakes on a tray. "Perhaps — half?"

"Oh heavens yes — more than half. Say — roughly — two-thirds."

"Really? Two-*thirds*? How long will it take to do the last third?"

"Oh, Kim, it's impossible to say."

"*Roughly. Try.*"

"Well — six months, then. *Roughly.* And then the fun will start."

"Yes, of course." Having the book published would be *much* more fun than writing it — that was hard work. "Do you think it will be difficult?"

"I just don't know yet. I hope not. It'll be very *slow*."

"Oh well." It didn't really matter, because the book would be finished then, and her father home. Six months! He might be back in *January* — that would make it two years altogether, which seemed about right for writing a book. She glanced down at the manuscript again. Scrawl and scribble, underlinings, crossings-out, and all totally illegible because her father had long ago invented his own speed-writing system; ordinary handwriting frustrated him, so much slower was it than his own lightning thought processes.

"Dad — are you sure you can *read* this?"

"It won't be much use if I can't, will it?"

"That's what's bothering me. Come here and I'll test you." She riffled through the pages. Oh blimey — they weren't even the same size. All sorts of paper, some with writing on both sides, some on one only. "You'll have to get a typewriter."

"I know — Kim, be careful! Don't get them out of order!" her father said with anguish.

"*Would* I. Now. Read me this word."

"A Party Member," her father said obediently.

"That little squiggle means *three* words?"

"Two. I don't bother with 'a' or 'the'. The Russians don't, so why should I? Neither word exists in the Russian language." Mr. Tate had taught himself Russian, many years before. He'd frequently offered to teach Kim, but Kim had taken one look at the alphabet and decided against it. "You really ought to learn a few words," her father said again, now. "Think how useful it might be."

"Oh, sure. When they invade us I'll be able to say 'Hello!'"

"You could learn to say: 'What a fine tank that is! And how nice it looks in my back garden!'"

"*Thanks* — what's this?" She picked up a photograph: four dark-haired girls, dressed in white.

"Oh yes — I meant to show you. Those are the Grand Duchesses — the daughters of the last Tsar. I thought you'd be interested because they were close in age, like you four — six years between oldest and youngest."

"Grand Duchess sounds like somebody of about ninety with a hooked nose and a bad temper."

"The sisters and daughters of the Tsars were always Grand Duchesses. I dare say some of them developed the

83

nose and the temper later on."

"Were they much like us? These four sisters?"

"Oh no. Very nice, sweet girls; never quarrelled, never argued. They were great friends."

"*Huh*. Which was the eldest? This one?"

"No — that's Tatiana. This one, Olga, was the eldest." Olga was a solemn, serious-faced girl; Tatiana looked a proud, superior sort of creature. "And this is Marie" — a chubby, pretty, smiling girl — "and this one's the youngest. Anastasia."

"I thought that was mercy killing."

"That's *euthan*asia."

"Grand Duchess Mercy Killing sounds terrific," Kim said. She rather liked the look of Anastasia, a cheeky, pert, lively-faced child. It must have been a wonderful life, being a Grand Duchess. Never any worries about money — and none of them would have gone to school, so no problems there either. "When was this taken?"

"Around 1910, I should think."

"Oh. Did the Tsar mind not having a boy?" Mr. and Mrs. Tate had said, separately, on several occasions, that *they* hadn't minded one bit, but these things were generally different for Tsars and the like.

"But he did have a boy. Three years after Anastasia was born, Nicholas and Alexandra — that's the Tsar and Tsarina — finally had a son. Alexis. They were overjoyed."

The names 'Nicholas and Alexandra' were familiar — hadn't that been the title of a film? Kim had never realized who they were. "Have you got a picture of Alexis?"

"No. I'm sorry. I could probably find you one. He was a lovely-looking child. He had haemophilia — do you know what that is?"

"I saw about it on television." Fascinating, it had been. "You can't stop bleeding, once you've started."

"That's right. The blood doesn't clot properly. Internal

84

bleeding — into a joint — causes the most excruciating agony. Poor Alexis. So much pain in such a short life."

"Oh — he *died* of it? How old was he?"

"Fourteen — but, Kim, he didn't die from the haemophilia! Don't you know about it? The Bolsheviks killed him. They killed all of them. The whole family."

"What? They killed the *children*? The girls too? But why?" She knew, instinctively, that this was going to be a ghastly thing. One of those haunting, nightmarish horrors — the sort of thing, in fact, that Kim could never leave alone.

"Because they were the Imperial Family, that was why. It was quite sufficient reason."

"How were they killed?"

"It was quite dreadful. Nicholas abdicated, you see — he was the last Romanov Tsar — and the family were held in captivity. They were moved around — they spent some time in Siberia. One night they were told they were to be moved again; they were to go downstairs to a basement room and wait. A firing squad came in and shot them all. And their servants, and the doctor. And the dog. But they missed Anastasia. She fainted, and when she came round she screamed. So they finished her off with bayonets."

Kim was silent for a moment, digesting this. At length she said: "But I can't understand *why*. Not the whole family. Not the children. They hadn't done anything. And why Nicholas? Was he a very wicked Tsar, then?"

"He wasn't wicked at all. He was a remarkably good, kind man, actually. Devoted to his family. His goodness was his downfall. Good men never seem to have been very successful at ruling Russia. If he'd been a tyrant and gone in for torture and mass murder he'd probably have been wildly popular."

"The Russians must be mad."

"They're quite impossible to understand. That's why I find them so engrossing, I suppose. You know, Alexandra

85

was the one who was really hated. The Tsarina. She was a German, and there was a monk called Rasputin . . . but that's another story."

"I can hardly believe it." She looked at the four young Grand Duchesses, so happy and innocent, so unaware of the bloody massacre that was to be their end.

"Some people *don't* believe it. They think that some, or all, of the family escaped; or that the whole thing was just staged. A number of people have turned up over the years, claiming to be one of the children. There was a very famous Anastasia. It's been relatively simple to prove them all fakes, though. Plenty of close relations, who knew the children well, survived the Revolution — the Tsar's sister Olga, his mother . . ."

"What do you think? Do you think they got away?"

"I haven't really gone into it thoroughly enough to judge. But I *think* they were slaughtered in that cellar. Still — there'll always be doubt."

Which added a certain piquancy, somehow. But what a story! Just wait till David heard about it . . ."Can I have the photo?"

"Yes, of course. I'll find you some books to read, if you're really interested. You're not going to *brood* about this, are you, Kim?"

"Yes. But don't worry, I'd have found out about it myself, sooner or later." The white dresses soaked with blood, the bodies riddled with bullets . . ."Let's talk about something else," she said abruptly. Time with her father was short and precious; she would gnaw over the Imperial Horror later.

"How about a game of chess, then?" They generally ended up playing chess. Kim wasn't all that keen. She couldn't give her father a proper game; they were too wildly ill-matched. And she would *much* rather talk. But her father enjoyed it so, and had few enough opportunities to play these days, so she said: "Yes, of course." Mr. Tate gave her two pawns' advantage, and beat her anyway.

Just before Kim left, which wasn't very late, because she had to walk McCluskey, and there was that fifteen-minute walk again, and two buses, her father gave her four pound notes, one for each of them. "And be sure to spend it on something you wouldn't have had otherwise," he told her firmly. So, on the way home, Kim called in to one of the ever-open Indian shops that sold *everything*, and bought three large punnets of strawberries. That carton of double cream was still sitting in the fridge, a reminder and a reproach; it was silly to waste it, and it would be much better eaten out of the way.

7

KIM AND McCLUSKEY GOT along very well. He was such a handsome creature, people were always pointing him out, or stopping to say 'Oh, *look!*' — and Kim rather enjoyed this. In the morning she took him down towards Chisholm Avenue and past her house, where Kerry, who had fallen in love with him instantly, gave him a great welcome — a good deal of fussing and patting, and a piece of digestive biscuit. But in the evenings Kim always made for the park and the graffiti wall; she was reading it like a serial, in daily instalments. The hot dog man was always there too; on one occasion McCluskey had disgraced himself against the left rear tyre of the van, but fortunately the man didn't notice. Soon, he and Kim were on grinning terms.

Kim was carefully memorizing all the best bits of graffiti; she planned to toss them out on suitable occasions, and dazzle people with her spontaneous wit. She particularly liked the Elvis series. This began innocently enough with:

ELVIS LIVES!

Beneath this, in another hand, was:

THEN WHY HAVE THEY BURIED HIM?

And then, the last word on the subject:

Then there were the 'RULES O.K.' set, which occupied a whole column, and were starting to overflow into a second:

ELIZABETH II RULES U.K.

AMNESIA RULES . . .ER . . .UM . . .

BULLFIGHTING RULES OLE!

LETHARGY RULEzzzzzz . . .

Some of them Kim couldn't understand.

EINSTEIN RULES RELATIVELY O.K.

(wasn't he the late developer?)

DYSLEXIA RULES K.O.

QUEENSBERRY RULES K.O.

She couldn't make these out at all. But this was her special favourite:

INDECISION RULES POSSIBLY

Kim did the evening walk between five and six; the morning stroll was generally finished by ten, which left both herself and Mrs. Hanrahan a goodly-sized chunk of day in the middle. Mrs. Hanrahan met her at the door, with McCluskey choke-chained and ready for the fray, except on Wednesday morning, when Kim found a note pinned to the front door: Kim — I've had to take to my bed with a very bad headacke. McC. is tied to a post in the back garden — please retie him when you return. S.H.

Kim knew about Mrs. Hanrahan's headaches; she had one every couple of months, and always had to take the day off school, so they must be pretty awful. What surprised her was the note itself: Mrs. Hanrahan, of all people, caught out in a spelling mistake. Kim removed the note and kept it, as written evidence.

Thursday evening marked the end of her first week of employment. "Come inside," said Mrs. Hanrahan. She was in trousers, again. Kim was learning to live with it. "I think it's about time we talked money, don't you?" Kim had been thinking exactly this for some time. She had no idea how much she was actually earning, and hadn't, somehow, liked to ask.

"Coffee?"

"Oh — yes, please." Kim did not in fact much like coffee, but it was always so unfriendly-sounding to refuse.

"Now. In these days nobody should be expected to work for less than a pound an hour. I don't believe in exploiting the young. Two half hour walks a day — seven pounds a week. Minus fifty pence for missing Friday morning. Plus a pound for being punctual, reliable and cheerful. Plus a pound for unsocial hours. Total, eight fifty. Does that suit you?"

"Thank you — that's great." As well as being her form mistress, Mrs. Hanrahan also taught Kim Maths; she almost expected to be told to calculate 6.9% of the total and express the result as a decimal, correct to three significant figures. Mrs. Hanrahan gave her a small brown envelope; she pocketed it with care. Her first pay packet.

"How are you getting along with the hound?"

"Oh, just fine." Kim grinned amiably at McCluskey. A dog with any sense of occasion would have thumped his tail with enthusiasm, or trotted over to lick her hand. McCluskey slept.

"Are you an animal-lover?"

"I'm an animal-*liker*," said Kim. "I don't go farther than that. I've got a sister absolutely batty about animals. Particularly him." She jerked a finger towards McCluskey. "She thinks he's the most gorgeous thing on this earth. She's dying to have one just like him."

"She's joining us next term, isn't she?"

"What? — Oh, no, that's another sister, Frances. The

90

animal one is Kerry. There's another one, too," she added, with elaboration.

"All school age? Where do the younger ones go? Priory Lane?"

"Anna does. Frances did." She hesitated — there was nothing but friendly interest in Mrs. Hanrahan's face, so she continued: "But Kerry doesn't go at all, much. She's got school phobia."

"Ah. And they can't find out the cause?"

"No."

Mrs. Hanrahan tapped her saucer thoughtfully. "Children have the most extraordinary reasons for disliking school. Does it make her ill?"

"Sick."

"It must be very worrying for your parents. How old is she?"

"Eight. Nearly nine. She's bright. But she's so far behind with her schoolwork, now. She hasn't even learned to read or write, yet. But they *know* she's bright. They think she's trying to hide it." She waited, hopefully, as if Mrs. Hanrahan might solve the problem just as easily and as confidently as she did mathematical monstrosities. But Mrs. Hanrahan, though clearly sympathetic, could suggest nothing. She did say, however, that she'd very much like to meet Kerry some time; if she was so attached to McCluskey, why didn't she come along with Kim on the walk now and then? Kim said she'd thought of that, but it hadn't seemed properly businesslike, making it into a family outing. Then the telephone rang. Mrs. Hanrahan's voice was notorious for the volume with which it could blast an idle third year; it carried through from the hall, and Kim heard — couldn't *help* hearing — "Didn't his wife go last month? Husbands never seem to last long on their own, do they? Out in Canley Green? I'll expect you back at about eight, then." Which put such a fascinating idea into Kim's head that she could hardly

91

wait to get home and check it out.

"Is that the paper with the poems and the dead people?" said Anna, seizing the *Thornton Gazette*.

Her mother groaned. "Here we go again. Kim always used to do this."

Anna smiled in happy anticipation and turned the pages busily until she reached In Memoriam. She had Made the Gesture; she had forgiven the family. None of them had been without blame. Anna had been furious with her mother for obvious reasons; furious with Kim for correctly predicting what would happen; furious with Frances for *failing* to predict what would happen; and furious with Kerry for existing. For a long while she hadn't spoken to any of them. Then, gradually, she began to notice that none of *them* was speaking to *her*, which was altogether different. So she was gracious and noble, and Made the Gesture. Particularly since her mother had bought her a very lovely new dressing gown, white with a lace inset and ribbon and little pink and orange flowers. Something like this usually happened, if she held out long enough. Just as long as they realized that between them they had destroyed her; that her life was, to all intents and purposes, over.

Kim was studying the Yellow Pages. First she looked up 'Undertakers' which told her to 'see Funeral Directors'. She turned back to the Fs and there it was. H.R. Hanrahan, 19 The Broadway, Thornton Cross. Now she came to think about it, she'd seen it, and noticed the name. It was right next to the Odeon. So it was true! Mrs. Hanrahan was married to an undertaker. How glorious! A husband who embalmed people. What conversations they must have in the evenings. She imagined Mrs. Hanrahan coming home from 2K, and Mr. Hanrahan coming home from his corpses, and the two of them agreeing that there wasn't a great deal of difference, really . . .

"What are you up to?" Mrs. Tate came and glanced over

her shoulder, intrigued by Kim's stifled laughter. "*Furniture*?"

"No — Funeral Directors."

"What? What on earth do you want with a Funeral Director? *I* don't know." She looked from Kim, buried amongst the undertakers, to Anna, deep In Memoriam. "What *is* going on here? I think I must have made some dreadful mistake when I was bringing you up. Where's Kerry? Digging a grave?"

"She went to have a bath," Frances said.

Anna cleared her throat. "*Quiet.*" She began to read, in mournful, lugubrious tones:

> " 'You were one of the very best
> Now you've gone to Eternal Rest.
> Every night I sit and weep
> Since the day you fell asleep.
> Thinking of you Bert.' "

"That's *terrible*," said Kim. "They've got worse since I used to read them."

"Anna," said her mother, "you really mustn't laugh at other people's grief."

> " 'We have no address to send our love,' "

read Anna,

> " 'We only know you're up above.
> God knows why he took you Bert.
> from Alf, Rene and the boys.' "

"Anna, stop it."

"Bert's well out of it," said Kim. "*He* hasn't got to read them. He probably killed himself from desperation. Cause of death: Suicide due to over-exposure to awful poems. Very sad. They rhymed him to death."

> " 'Your laughing face is with us still,
> Oh Bert, we . . .' "

"ANNA!"

"If I die," said Frances, "you're all to promise not to write verses. I won't be here to answer back."

"Of course we won't," said Kim. "We'll forget you absolutely. Shame really — I could write some lovely ones . . ."

"Go on then," said Anna. "Make one up now. I bet you can't."

"For you? A pleasure. To the Late Anna Tate . . ."

"*Not* for me. Do one for Bert."

"I'd have thought he's got enough already . . .oh, all right." She thought for a few moments, then nodded, and said solemnly:

> "Well, Bert.
> Did it hurt?"

"Is that all? But that was awful. It wasn't enough! It . . ."

"It was perfect. Short and to the point. It's just what everyone wants to ask the dead anyhow."

"*Enough*," said Mrs. Tate. "Nobody is to mention death again *all evening*."

Anna looked sadly at Birthday Memories. She hadn't even *started* to read those out yet. "I'm going to wash and change," she said, getting up. "I feel *sticky*." This fooled nobody; the new dressing gown was about to get its first public airing. Mrs. Tate reached for the paper.

"Now perhaps I can have a look at the jobs. That *was* what I bought it for."

"I've looked already," Kim said. "There's nothing there. It's a dead loss. *Sorry*, Mum. It just slipped out."

It was true enough, though. There were plenty of suitable vacancies in central London, but Mrs. Tate refused even to consider commuting. It would mean leaving at the crack of dawn, and not getting home till seven. It was out of the question. So she had limited her search to Thornton Cross, Canley and Canley Green; and there was just nothing. The

94

ads under 'Shops and Stores' were all 'School Leaver wanted' . . . 'Part-time Sales Assistant' . . . 'Young Person wanted by Busy Newsagent' . . . there had been one that said 'Manageress Wanted for Jeweller's. Must have experience' — but a phone call had established that they required experience of managing a jeweller's, not of running a handicrafts department. It was all very depressing. Mrs. Tate had written off about a number of jobs in other fields, but had not as yet received so much as a reply from any of them. Job hunting wasn't fun at all. And signing on the dole must have been infinitely worse; she wouldn't even talk about that.

And then there was the car. This secret had proved quite impossible to keep; Mrs. Tate had no sooner looked at the cheque than she said: "Oh God, he must have sold the car." Kim wasn't sure if she'd guessed that he'd also given up his job, nor was she certain if this, too, was a secret. She said nothing; if he wanted her mother to know, he could tell her himself. She wished he would. So many secrets. It was starting to be impossible to talk to either parent about the other. There was something almost farcical about it: both of them jobless, and neither willing that the other should know it. Thank heavens for the good news about the progress of the novel. Two-thirds finished; Mrs. Tate had been flabbergasted. It had gone a long way towards easing the blow of the car.

Mrs. Tate surveyed the Situations Vacant. It didn't take very long. "You're right, Kim, I'm afraid. Oh — blow it. Next week there'll be something. Perhaps the manageress of Crafty will decide to go into a convent, and I'll take over."

"Well — at least I'm earning something," Kim said. "Even if it isn't enough to make much difference." She had been thoroughly confused by Mrs. Hanrahan's payment system. She *thought* she was making nine pounds a week, but it seemed that there might be deductions made if she failed to show up on time, or wasn't cheerful. Or had this been a joke? Kim and her mother had squabbled quite seriously over the division of the money; Mrs. Tate wanted Kim to keep half of it, which Kim absolutely refused to do. They eventually negotiated a settlement of two pounds fifty for Kim, six fifty for her mother.

"Of course it makes a difference. It's a great help."

"If the worst came to the *very* worst," Kim said, knowing that it wouldn't, "we'd just sell the Renton jewels, that's all."

"They're sold already," said her mother. Seeing the expressions on her daughters' faces, she faltered briefly, but continued, with a determined smile: "We really couldn't have *lived* if I hadn't. Well, we might have lived, but we'd have been counting every penny. And I'd have had to go and ask what beastly *Benefits* we were entitled to." She banged her hand on the table. "I wasn't going to *do* that. Means tests. No *way*. And why should we have to count the pennies? It would have been awful. Never an outing to the cinema — no money for Christmas or birthdays — no treats, ever, no surprises, no *fun* — well, that wasn't good enough! Not for *my* children."

"Even the diamond and sapphire necklace?" was all Kim could think of to say.

"That," said her mother, "was the first to go."

And she'd said not one word! All this time! "Well, doesn't matter. At least that'll save us arguing over who's to get it. Right, Frances?" But it was obvious that, to Frances, it wasn't right at all. Her face told its own story. She *minded*. How strange. Kim had never thought that Frances cared tuppence about jewels.

"Look, Frances," said Mrs. Tate, who could read a face just as well as Kim could, "it's a lot worse for me. You've hardly ever *seen* them. I grew up with them. If I can bear it, so can you." And so — that was that. The Renton heritage no longer existed.

Kim said, sensibly, "What you've never had you can't miss, and it never seems that we've really *had* them" — but, of course, it wasn't that simple. The jewels had represented Security: a security that seemed suddenly much more important and desirable now that it was no longer there. "Why are you telling us now, when you never did before?"

"Well, it's different now; now I know that this isn't going on for much longer. Before — when it was indefinitely — and the jewels running out — you must see that I wouldn't have wanted to say anything." Footsteps sounded on the stairs. "Change the subject," she said hastily. In danced Anna; she began to twirl, then remembered, just in time, that she had changed because she was sticky. She walked casually to an armchair.

"Very nice, darling," said her mother. Anna beamed, and leapt up again immediately, all pink and gold and clean and smelling of talcum powder — Kerry had knocked the powder over and was still in the bathroom, trying to clean up the mess — and, belatedly, twirled.

"Lovely," said Frances, subdued. Anna frowned; this just wasn't good enough. Four words, between the three of them!

"It fits *just right*," she said, as, apparently, nobody else was going to comment on the fact.

"Yes," said her mother. "It *really* suits you, Anna. Don't you think so" — she was about to add 'Frances' but, under the circumstances, changed her mind and appealed to Kim instead. "Don't you think so, Kim?"

"You look just terrific, Anna," Kim said, and added, thoughtfully: "Like . . . like . . ."

"Yes?"

"Like a dog that's just been wormed."

"Did you *have* to?" asked Frances.

They were in bed; Kim was lying on her side facing the wall, and studying, once again, her photograph of the daughters of the Tsar. She had read about them now, and had discovered that her snap judgments had been remarkably accurate: Tatiana *was* a haughty madam, devoted to her mother the Tsarina; Olga a very nice, hard-working girl, fond of reading; Marie was sweet-tempered, kind and lazy, with a big heart; Anastasia a vivacious clown. Kim had found other photographs, and now knew their faces from all angles. She sometimes imagined how they would all get along together, if the Romanovs lived next door to the Tates, in Chisholm Avenue. Marie and Frances would be great friends, no doubt; Tatiana would be rather like Bryony; Olga would be pleasant and friendly and helpful, but would seem rather grown-up. And Anna and Anastasia would fight like mad.

This feeling, that she *knew* the fated Grand Duchesses, made their hideous murder all the more agonizing. Especially now that she had discovered how the bodies had been disposed of; the process had involved saws, axes, fire, sulphuric acid and a mine shaft. And Anastasia! For the life of her Kim could not stop thinking of Anastasia's last moments, when she regained consciousness after her faint. What had she seen? What had she heard? Did she *realize*? Desperately, Kim hoped not; for, if she had, it was horror enough to wake the souls of all the dead, and Anastasia's soul was probably still screaming to this day. It made the Tates' troubles seem somewhat trivial.

"What did you say?" She half-turned towards Frances, rather irritably; she hadn't heard the words, but she had grasped the tone of them.

"I said, did you *have* to say that to Anna? You *always* do it, don't you? Couldn't you just once say the truth? You know she looked nice. It wouldn't hurt to say so."

"*She* knows she looks nice," said Kim, not liking this at

all; who was Frances, to give her lectures? "She knows it all too well. She doesn't need any encouragement from me."

"You're just beastly to her," Frances continued, stubbornly. "She is your *sister*."

"You're a fine one to talk. What about Dad? He's your *father*. And you can't even be bothered to go and see him."

Frances sat bolt upright. "No I won't go and see him!"

"Well? Why not?"

And Frances — Frances! — said: "Because I think men who go off and leave their wives ought to be *shot*."

Kim blinked. "What? You don't know what you're talking about."

"Oh yes I do. I mean it. Going off and leaving Mum to do all the working and the worrying for *two* parents — and making her sell her precious jewels that were all she had! — and *he's* just doing what he wants to do! He's *enjoying* himself. Just sitting around doing stupid puzzles and reading stupid books and nobody to bother him or interrupt him . . ."

"He's working on something that's going to make money for all of us in the long run. Can't you understand that?"

"He's enjoying himself! *Playing games*. And what about us? He doesn't give a damn what's happening to us!"

"He does! How would you know! You won't go and see him! It's ages since you even spoke to him!"

"I just *know*. Do you honestly believe he'd come back now? If we said we were in trouble and we begged him to come back tomorrow, do you think he would?"

"Frances, he's writing a book! He's coming back when it's finished! And it nearly *is* finished . . ."

"I don't care about his stupid book! He ought to be here! He ought to be working so that we've got enough money and Mum doesn't have to sell things!"

Kim almost said: "He *is* working" but remembered just in time that he wasn't, not any more.

99

"You're blind about him! You always have been! You don't see what's happening. And you're supposed to be the one that's so clever. You're *blind*. Well, I'm not. And I *don't want to see him*."

"All right. So you don't." Frances might be eleven, and supposedly sensible, but just at the moment she was behaving like a silly, petulant baby. All because of those jewels. Well, Kim wasn't going to rise to it. She would be *mature*. Frances would learn in time. "You see what I mean, then? You're the one who doesn't know how to behave to members of her own family. Not me."

"You want to bet on that? All right. I'll tell you something else, then. I'll tell you why it is that Janice won't come here any more. She can't stand listening to you and Anna. On at each other the whole time. She *said* to me — 'Aren't Kim and Anna awful to each other? I feel terrible. I never know where to look.' *That's* how you make people feel. She's too embarrassed to come here."

Janice? Chubby, good-natured, pleasant little Janice had said *that*? About *her*? Kim had always thought that Janice rather admired her . . . "Janice is a stupid little twit," she said angrily. "All sisters get at each other. It's *human*. It's *normal*. I can't help it if you're so *super*human and *saintly* . . ."

"But you two never stop! If it was just now and again the things you say might be funny. But not *all the time*. And don't you *dare* to be rude about Janice."

"I'll say what I like about Janice. Or anybody else. And you know how Anna talks. It's awful! She has to be told. She's . . ." Kim was torn between 'precocious' and 'obnoxious' — which was the word she wanted? Frances didn't wait to find out.

"Only when you're there she talks like that! She's quite different when you're not. She does it to get you going, half the time. She *likes* a row. And you always rise to it, don't you?"

"She's the one that sets it off!"

"*She's* only seven. You're old enough to know better."

"You!" Kim said, furiously. "You think she's perfect! You can't see any wrong in her! And you've got the nerve to call *me* blind!"

"I'm not blind. I know what Anna is. She's selfish and vain and bossy. And I like her anyway! And she'll probably grow out of it. You never think about what else she is. She's bright and funny and she's lively and she's got masses of personality. And she's brave. And she's popular. She's got loads of friends, which is more than *you've* got. And she's got more confidence than you'll ever have. She *believes* in herself. What's wrong with that? Are you jealous, or what?"

"Oh, now you're joking." She was sick and tired of being told that people were jealous of Anna.

"Well, then, stop putting her down. You ought to listen to the two of you. Trying to catch each other out. Trying to beat each other all the time. You're ever so much alike really. In *lots* of ways. Yes you are! So if you despise her so much you can just despise yourself too, because you're no better. And everyone else gets tired of listening to the both of you. It's just boring. And you've driven my best friend away. So there you are."

8

KIM WOKE JUST BEFORE eight the next morning, and dressed and slipped downstairs, while the rest of the house slept on. She couldn't be bothered with fancy cooking (tea and toast); instead she cut a hunk of bread and cheese and ate it with a glass of fresh orange juice. She switched the radio on, softly, for company.

A row with Frances was almost unheard of; it was very unsettling. Particularly such a one-sided row; *Frances* had had the row, Kim had just lain there and been rowed at. She only hoped it wasn't going to be one of those rows that *linger*; she hated that. It was so pointless. Frances having the nerve to say *she* was blind! Frances went on about Anna as if she were an angel at the very least, and probably in line for promotion to archangel at any moment. Kim fetched the dictionary, looked up 'precocious' and 'obnoxious' and discovered that either word would have done excellently. Anna would be unbearable but for Kim's sisterly influence. Actually, she was unbearable anyway.

And Janice? Janice refusing to come to the Tates' house because of *Kim*? She didn't believe it. But the fact remained that Janice didn't come any more, which was pretty rotten for Frances. Well, she'd have to think about this one. She'd try to *watch* herself and Anna — not that she believed a word of Frances's twaddle, but it would be as well to find out for herself. And in the meantime, she would Make the Gesture. Mrs. Tate was a great believer in this. It was a brilliant tactic, she said. It made the adversary feel uneasy, and put you in a very strong position. Kim thought of an excellent Gesture. She would apologize to Anna. She would tell her that she looked stunning in the dressing gown — and would she like Kim to take her to the library? A *combined* Gesture. A *multiple* Gesture. And possibly Anna would faint from the shock, and they'd all have a nice peaceful day.

So that was settled; she sat back, and began to listen to the radio, which had until then been little more than a buzz in the background.

"So I'll just repeat that one more time . . ." said Bill Maloney, who had been yattering away about something or other for ages . . . "if *you* would like to try your hand at being a Kidsline presenter for a day, just ring this number." He played a jingle; a musical phone number. "Remember — we're looking for young people with a nice speaking voice and *loads* of personality. And I must remind you — today's your very last chance. So get dialling now! The phone lines will be open till midday. And now here's an oldie from Abba on your cuddly breakfast show to take us up to the news headlines . . ."

Kim reached over and switched off. Two things were instantly clear. Anna didn't know a thing about it. And if Kim didn't tell her, she never would. Now, here was an interesting situation. What to do?

She'd be impossible to live with if she got on Kidsline, said Kim A.

She's impossible to live with as it is, countered Kim B.

I didn't write the number down, said Kim A.

You *know* the number, said Kim B. You've heard that jingle a hundred times. Forty-four twenty four eighty-one two two.

But I've already *decided* on a Gesture, Kim A pointed out.

The bigger the Gesture, Kim B answered cleverly, the greater the advantage to the maker.

What's she ever done for me?

JANICE, said Kim B, and both Kims went off to collect McCluskey, still arguing and contradicting each other. It seemed a good idea to change the routine and walk to the park rather than past the Tates' house. I'M IN TWO MINDS ABOUT SCHIZOPHRENIA, said the wall, nastily.

"You're early," said Anna, when Kim got back.

"So I am. Where's Frances?" She rather hoped Frances wasn't up, just yet . . .

"Still in bed. What are you looking at me like that for?"

"Just wondering," said Kim, sitting down by Kerry and accepting a cup of tea from her mother. "Wondering whether to tell you that if you ring 4424 8122 you might learn something to your advantage, that's all. There. Now I *have* told you."

Anna eyed her mistrustfully. "What d'you mean by that?" She wasn't going to be caught out. It was probably the number of that funerals person Kim had been looking up — or Rentokil — or a *dog-wormer* . . . "*I'm* not going to ring any number."

"That's a shame," Kim said tranquilly. "Because if you had, you might have ended up helping Bill Maloney to present Kidsline one day . . . still. You know best."

"Is this true, Kim?" Mrs. Tate asked, since Anna, apparently, had been rendered totally speechless.

"M-hm. I didn't hear all of it — just that anyone who wants a go is to ring before midday."

Anna gazed at her mother. She just knew that she was going to say she couldn't. All anybody thought of these days was finding out what Anna most wanted to do, and then

104

stopping her from doing it.

"Well, off you go then, Anna. You know where the phone is."

"Can I? *Oh*!" She ran out into the hall, only to return a second later, wailing: "But I don't remember the number!"

"Hang on," Kim said, "and I'll write it down for you."

"Hurry *up*, Kim! It's nearly midday! It'll be . . . "

"It's *ten* to *ten*. There you are." She handed a piece of paper to Anna, with a sweet, loving smile; Anna goggled and fled, glancing nervously over her shoulder at Kim, who smiled on, relentlessly.

"Are you all right?" Kerry tapped her arm, much puzzled.

"What? Oh yes, I'm fine. Hush. I want to listen."

"It's engaged," called Anna.

"Then keep trying, darling," said her mother. Anna hung up and redialled. Still engaged. Ping. Dial. Ping. Dial. The three in the kitchen listened, mesmerized. Kerry was keeping count. Ping. Dial. "How many's that?" hissed her mother. "Fourteen," said Kerry. Ping.

"Anna? Shall I take over for a while?"

"NO," said Anna, dialling. Engaged. Ping . . .What would she do if she never got through? There were only two hours left till midday! Perhaps they'd taken the phone off the hook! She would die! Ping. Dial. Ping . . . No! It was ringing! "It's ringing!" she shrieked. "Twenty-three," said Kerry.

"Radio Thames. Can I help you?"

"Oh, yes, please. I want to be a presenter on Kidsline." This was really exciting. She was talking to a *radio station*.

"Hello," said a different voice. "Can I have your name, please?"

"Anna. Anna Victoria Tate."

'Well, Anna, I'm Bridget Munroe. I'm the producer of Kidsline. Now, what I'd like you to do for me is to talk about yourself for a while. Just tell me about your home, your family, your school — anything you like. Try not to stop — keep talking. I know it's difficult, but have a go."

Difficult? Talking about herself? "Well, I live in Canley, in Chisholm Avenue, and I've got three older sisters, and a mother, and a father but he's not here just at the moment. We've got a very nice house, three bedrooms though we really could do with four, and a garden back and front. I've got long blonde hair and blue eyes and a few freckles, but not *too* many. I look best in pink; that's my favourite colour. My school's called Priory Lane, it's about five minutes' walk from here, and my teacher is Mrs. Langley, and last term I was Flowers Monitor and I won the prize for the best handwriting. I've got fourteen friends. I like singing and reading, and going to the pictures and watching television, and . . ."

"Thanks, Anna, that was fine. Now I'd like you to read me something. Anything that's handy. It doesn't matter what it is." Anna looked around frantically; all she could see was the telephone directory. It would have to do. She cleared her throat, and read to Bridget, in her very best voice, the instructions for obtaining the Fire Brigade, Police, Ambulance or Coastguard. "Was that all right?"

"Yes — actually that was very good. Why do you want to be on Kidsline?" she asked suddenly.

"Because I want to be famous." Why else? Mrs. Tate and Kim, hearing this, groaned, deeply and simultaneously. Now she'd done it. She'd blown it. She should have said: "Because it's such a good programme" — or words to that effect — *any*thing but what she *had* said . . .

"Good for you," said Bridget. "You're the twenty-fourth person I've spoken to this morning, and the first to give me a sensible answer."

"What did the others say?"

"Most of them said: 'I dunno really' or 'Nothing else to

106

do, is there?' One said: 'I'll have to ask my Mum.' So — good for you. Well, Anna, I think we'll have you along for a trial run, all right? To see how you get on in the studio. I just have to take down a few details. Name, address, phone number . . ." Anna reeled off this information, in a daze of delight. She was going to be a radio star! She would be very famous indeed! "And how old are you?"

"Seven. Nearly eight."

"*Seven* — but, Anna, I thought you were nine or ten! Surely you heard Bill say that we couldn't consider anybody under nine?"

"You . . ." Not considering anybody . . . Anna's stomach revolved. It had been a trick! It had! It was the meanest thing Kim had ever done! To get her to ring up . . . and she *wasn't old enough* . . .

"Anna? Are you there? Look, dear. I'm so sorry . . ."

"If you thought I was nine," Anna said, wildly, desperately, "so will anybody! I must *sound* nine. Oh, please, Bridget. I want to do it so much . . ."

Bridget was silent for a moment. Then she said: "Hold on a minute, will you? I want to talk to Bill." Anna caught the words: "Bill, there's a little girl here . . ." and then a hand was put over the receiver at the other end, and she heard no more. But it made no difference; she knew what Bridget would be saying. There was a girl on the line who was only seven but she was much much better than any of the other twenty-three people who'd rung up and if they didn't give her a chance they would be ruining a brilliant career and they would regret it for the rest of their lives. So they must make an exception, in this case . . .

"Anna? Hello, it's Bridget again. Well — we think we may be willing to make an exception for you; willing to give you a trial, anyway. I can't promise that you'll make it on to the air. We decided on the age limit of nine, you see, because Bill wasn't too keen on the thought of anyone younger than that being let loose in the studio. But I managed to convince him that you sounded sensible." Wonderful, marvellous Bridget. In years to come, when Anna was asked how she had first come to put her foot on the road to glittering stardom, she would say: "Well, there was a lady called Bridget Munroe" . . . "Oh, thank you, Bridget! Did you really talk to Bill Maloney?" A famous disc jockey! Somebody had talked about her to a famous . . ."Yes, of course," said Bridget, sounding amused. "He's standing about ten feet away from me. Bill!" Her voice faded slightly. "Say hello to Anna, will you?" And a voice — a *familiar* voice — called: "Hello, Anna!" She was on speaking terms with a famous disc jockey! "Hello, Bill!" she shouted back at once. Bridget relayed this to Bill; Anna heard general laughter down the line.

"Well, we'll see you on Friday, then," Bridget said, still half-chuckling. "Can I have a word with your mother, please? To make the arrangements?"

"MUM!" bellowed Anna; Mrs. Tate came out and took the receiver; Anna hovered. Mrs. Tate shooed her away; Anna took a step backwards and hovered there. But Bridget was doing all the talking. All her mother was saying was: "Yes. Of course . . . that's what I thought . . . yes, that'll be fine . . . I'm sure she will" — will *what*? — "right, then. Goodbye."

"*What did she say?*"

"*All* she said was where to go, and when, and how to get there. That was *it*."

"Ooooh." Anna hugged herself in delicious ecstasy — then she saw Kim, and *remembered*."You beast! You pig! You thought you were going to trick me! I knew you wouldn't smile like that otherwise! I . . ."

"Anna," said her mother. "What are you talking about?"

"It was only open to people aged nine and over! And she made me ring up and she thought I'd make a fool of myself

108

but they made an exception for me because I was so *good* . . ."

"Don't be such an idiot, Anna. I told you, I didn't hear all of what he said." So *this* was the thanks you got . . ."I just caught the very end of it, that's all. And you'd better be careful what you say, or another time I shan't bother."

"Quite right," said her mother. "Anna, you haven't thanked Kim yet."

Thank her? For playing a fiendish mean trick?

"Anna?"

"Thank you, Kim." Anna said, with exaggerated politeness.

"But it was a pleasure, Anna. And I'm so glad that you're going to be on the radio." Kim smiled the loving smile again; Anna shrank back. She couldn't stand this. It was terrible! What was *wrong* with Kim today? Perhaps she *hadn't* been trying to trick her . . . that would be even worse . . .

"*Possibly* going to be on the radio," said their mother.

"Of course I will," Anna said. "They couldn't say no now. Could they?"

"Well, actually, it's not very likely. The phone call was the real hurdle. Bridget said that most people got no further than that. As long as you don't faint with terror in the studio, you should be O.K."

"You didn't tell me Bridget said that!"

"Well, I've told you now, haven't I? Probably a terrible mistake."

"What did Anna do that was right?" asked Kim. "I mean, how come she was one of the few to get past the phone call?"

"She *talked*, didn't she? She didn't stammer, or dry up, or say 'er — um — you know' — and she reads nicely, of course. But it was the flow of words that seems to have done the trick. Silence always sounds terrible on radio. It doesn't seem to matter what you *say*, as long as you keep *talking*. Well, that's the impression I get listening to most of those

109

disc jockeys." She caught sight of the clock, and frowned. "Where's Frances? Spending the day in bed?"

"She's up," said Kerry. All that shouting would have woken anybody, even Frances. "I heard her go into the bathroom just now."

"And not before time."

"She doesn't know anything about it," said Anna, happily; she would be able to tell the whole story right through from start to finish. She paused, expecting some caustic comment from Kim. But Kim was still smiling at her benevolently, with tender affection. Anna felt very uneasy indeed.

9

"YOU MUSTN'T WORRY," Kim said. "She's really nice."

Kerry, leading McCluskey along on the return journey from the park, looked far from convinced. It was not the first time that she'd accompanied Kim on the walk, but this was Thursday, and pay day, and they'd more than likely be asked inside.

"Just forget she's a teacher. She's off duty now. Think of her as the person who owns McCluskey. Well, for the time being."

"I could always go home," Kerry said, hopefully.

"You'll do no such thing. She wants to meet you."

"What?" Kerry stood stock still. "Why?"

"Because I've told her how nice you are, that's why." Kerry squinted sidelong at her; they both giggled.

"Is she your last year's form teacher or next year's?"

"Both, actually. In our school we have the same form mistress from the second year right up to the fifth."

Kerry didn't comment on this. Instead she said: "Aren't you going to miss McCluskey, Kim, when his people come and take him back?"

"Not half as much as I'll miss the money," Kim said wickedly.

"Oh, *Kim*." Kerry rubbed the dog's head gently. "Of

course you'll miss him. You couldn't help it. Kim?"

"Yes?"

"Would it cost an awful lot of money, to have an Old English sheepdog?"

"It would, Kerry. Really it would. At least a hundred pounds to buy the dog, and even if we could manage that we couldn't afford to keep it. You have to spend a fortune to feed a dog that size. Perhaps in a few years' time you'll be able to have one. When the money from Dad's book starts coming in. I'm sure he'll buy you a dog."

Kerry pulled a face. It all sounded very, very far ahead.

"I'd buy you one tomorrow if I had the money," Kim said. "You know I would. And I know that doesn't make it any better. Right — here we are. Can you drink a cup of coffee, if she offers you one?"

"I like coffee," said Kerry.

"Do you? But you never drink it at home! When have you tried it?"

"*Nobody* drinks it at home. I would if they did. I had a cup when I was out with Mum. I thought it was lovely."

"My sister's a secret coffee drinker," Kim told Mrs. Hanrahan, a few moments later. "And I've only just found it out."

"I can see we're going to get on, Kerry." Mrs. Hanrahan was indeed making them coffee. "I'm a great coffee drinker myself." Kerry was dreadfully nervous, Kim noticed gloomily. She was practically trembling. Perhaps it had been a mistake to bring her after all. If she managed to speak a total of twenty words before they left, she would be doing well.

Mrs. Hanrahan appeared unaware that anything was amiss. "How do you like it?" she was asking Kerry. "Weak? Strong? Milky?"

"Um — milky." Well, that was two words, anyhow.

"Would you bring the milk over? I've put it out on the

112

slab." Kerry went over and picked up the bottle — at that instant Kim thought: she's going to drop it. The next second, Kerry dropped the bottle. The crash seemed unreasonably loud. Kerry leaped backwards and clapped her hand over her mouth, looking from one to the other of them in almost desperate apology.

"I'm *sorry*," Kim said, in a fluster. "She didn't . . . let me clean it up . . . I . . ."

"Don't fuss," said Mrs. Hanrahan, calmly. "Stop looking so anguished, both of you. These things happen." Which wasn't what she'd said that time Nicky French had knocked a vase off her desk . . ."Sit down, Kim. I'll see to it in a jiffy." She brushed the glass rapidly into a dustpan, and mopped up the milk. "Now, just watch for any stray bits of glass, that's all. And don't *worry* about it. There was less than half a pint left in it, and I've plenty more. Kerry, will you bring me another bottle, please? Yes, a full one. No, of course you won't drop this one as well . . .There you are, you see? No trouble at all. Anyone can have an accident."

Kerry looked at her for a long while and said: "But not *every day*!"

"Don't you believe it. I was exactly the same, at your age. Never a day passed without some disaster. My parents used to breathe a great sigh of relief when I'd got the day's breakage over with."

"Really?"

"And I grew out of it. Well — I improved. So will you."

This was a very different Mrs. Hanrahan from the one Kim saw at school, and she suddenly decided that she liked her, very much indeed. Not many people would go to such lengths to reassure a child — and she'd done it so cleverly! Kerry was looking calmer already. All might yet be well, so long as Mrs. Hanrahan didn't spoil it by asking her questions, about school, and all that . . . surely she wouldn't be so stupid.

Mrs. Hanrahan wasn't stupid. She settled Kerry with her cup of coffee, and then turned to Kim. "I was looking through the form lists last night, and I happened to notice that I'll be teaching your sister next year."

"Oh, that's good." Was it? More to the point, did Mrs. Hanrahan think so? Then she realized what Mrs. Hanrahan had said. "Form lists? You mean that the new first years have already been put into forms?"

"Yes. Why?"

"Well, it's just that Frances — the only thing that seems to be bothering her about starting at Thornton Park is that she wants so much to be in the same form as her friend Janice. They've been really inseparable, you know, for years . . ."

"And you wondered if I might be persuaded to leak the information?"

Fortune favoured the brave. "Yes. I did."

Mrs. Hanrahan thought about it for a moment. "I can't see that it would do any harm. What's Janice's surname?"

"Maudsley."

"Hang on a minute." She left the room.

"I like her," said Kerry.

"*Do* you? Well, good. I told you she was nice. Didn't you believe me?"

"No," said Kerry. Mrs. Hanrahan returned.

"Well, they're lucky. Both in IR, with Mr. Hughes." This last fact was not so lucky, but Frances and Janice could find that out for themselves. "At one time," Mrs. Hanrahan went on, "we did try to keep people together in the first year, if they were really close friends, but we don't bother now. For one thing it's not always possible to find out who the close friends are; for another, people often grow out of each other very quickly, when they arrive at secondary school."

"I doubt if those two will," Kim said, well pleased. Frances was still being very stand-offish — perhaps, in all honesty, so was Kim — but this news, and the fact that Kim had gone to such great lengths to find it out — by the time Frances heard about it they'd be great lengths, anyhow — ought to go some way towards putting things right.

"What about *your* friend, Kim? Is he not back yet?"

"David? He's coming back tomorrow, some time."

"Am I right to say 'friend' as opposed to 'boyfriend'?"

"Of course," Kim said, shocked. "We've lived next door to each other all our lives."

"Well, you never know. They seem to arrive from primary school with a boy on their arms, these days. And the boy always looks so uncomfortable . . ." Kerry laughed at that, and Mrs. Hanrahan winked at her. "What do you find to do, in these long holidays?"

"It is a long time . . . I expect we'll be going cycling, when David's back. We usually do. We *were* going to Warren Hill, but something kept happening to stop us. I'll tell you what the trouble is with school holidays. So many things are shut up in school where you can't get at them. Like the tennis courts. They just *sit* there for six weeks, with the gates locked, and loads of people like me would love to be able to use them."

"It does seem a waste. But I suppose there are Reasons. Somebody would have to be there to let you in — and there'd have to be some checking system. We couldn't have just anybody walking in off the streets."

"I suppose not." Kim was a little perplexed; there seemed to be no limits to Mrs. Hanrahan's friendliness. It was all very *nice* — but coffee, and bringing Kerry, and leisurely chat — it was going a great deal further than Kim would have thought necessary, or even normal, under the circumstances. All the time she was half-expecting a very polite brush-off: to be put back in her place, in fact. But it didn't come. The danger, Kim felt, was that the relaxed atmosphere might lull her into forgetting to whom she was

115

speaking; she might say something outrageous. She'd have to be very careful.

"You're interested in sport, aren't you? I seem to remember that you did rather well on Junior Sports Day."

"That's another thing. I've been dying to practise the high jump. I was coming on so well. And I want to *win* it next year, if I can . . . but all the athletics equipment is locked up in school, and there's nothing I can use. It's maddening."

"It must be. Isn't it a good thing, then, that the Thorn Centre will be so near?"

"Oh, *that*." The Thorn Sports Centre had been due to open eighteen months ago. It still wasn't finished. Kim could hardly remember a time when they *hadn't* been building it, so long had the process taken. First there had been the problem with the foundations. They sank. So another site was found, and they began again. Then the builders went on strike. Two weeks after their return, the electricians went on strike, and the builders came out again in sympathy. The Centre became a local joke: rather a bitter joke, since the ratepayers were providing most of the money. The estimated date of completion was moved forward, and forward again. It was all very British. People began to express doubt as to whether the building would actually be opened during their lifetime. Kim, to whom it would have been heaven on earth to have a sports centre just ten minutes' walk from her home, had been so often disappointed that now she was always very scornful about the Centre, as if trying to convince it that she didn't *care*. "By the time they open that, the only exercise I'll be getting is hobbling along to the post office to collect my pension."

"Oh no, it really is opening this time. At the beginning of September. And one of the royal family — I can't remember which — is coming to open it *officially* in October. That seems to be the usual order of doing things, nowadays. Didn't you get a sort of leaflet through the letter

116

box?"

"No. I hadn't heard a thing. But — the beginning of September! That's only a month away. It's really definite, then? That's fantastic."

"I've got the leaflet somewhere. It's a pink thing." She went and rummaged in a drawer. "You can have it if you like. I can't understand why you didn't get one. I do remember that indoor athletics was one of the facilities mentioned. You'll be able to practise high jumping all year round. Here you are."

"*Oh.*" It was too big to be called a leaflet; it was more of a booklet, and it was called the Thorn Centre News. "Look at this, Kerry! No — listen, and I'll read it to you. There's going to be badminton, squash, table tennis, a swimming pool and skating rink, indoor athletics, trampolines, a climbing wall . . . they've got cricket nets, basketball . . . they're going to do judo and gymnastics and five-a-side football . . . social activities and events, visiting display teams . . .oh, this is fantastic."

"I wouldn't mind trying a trampoline," Kerry said surprisingly.

"Well, so you shall . . . we can get one of these family memberships — that'll get us all in for a whole year." Except — they wouldn't be able to afford it. Oh, they'd manage somehow. There had to be enough money for a thing like this. They could sell Anna.

Anna recognized the pink booklet straight away.

"We had one of those," she said. "It came through the door."

"Did we? Then why hasn't anybody seen it?"

"I took it to read. It was such a nice colour."

"You took it . . . and you didn't *tell* us? The Thorn Centre opening in a month and you didn't *say*?"

"I didn't say I *read* it. I *took* it to read. I forgot about it. I can't even remember where I put it now. Never mind. I can read that one instead."

"You keep your sticky paws off!" Anna was relieved; this was more like it. Kim still smiled that sweet smile now and then; Anna dreaded it. It made her flesh creep. "You're not going to lose this one too. I want to show it to Mum. She'll be interested; there's lots to read in it. Advertisements, even."

"Poems and dead people?"

"Nobody's died there yet, you fool. It's not *opened*. When people start to fall off the climbing wall, then they might. It's going to be a monthly publication."

"In loving memory of our darling Paul, who fell off the wall." Anna said, and smiled with deep contentment.

"Cricket nets!" said David, pleased. "Now that *is* sensible of them." The Holders had arrived at the crack of dawn; now it was half past one, and he and Kim had adjourned to the roofs. They had much to discuss. The Tate house had, all day, been revolving around Anna's visit to Radio Thames; she had changed her clothes four times before finally satisfying herself that she looked good enough to appear on the radio. She and Mrs. Tate had just left, Mrs. Tate somewhat apprehensive and Anna bouncing, assuring her that there was nothing to worry about at all. It would be perfectly all right; it would be marvellous. "I hope so," said Mrs. Tate, anticipating the scenes that would follow if it wasn't.

David had brought presents for everybody, including Mrs. Tate; Kim's was a beautiful road sign that said: DANGER — LOW-FLYING NUNS. It had rained, he said; it had rained on him every single day. He was convinced he had shrunk. Next year perhaps they'd take his advice and go to Austria.

He was delighted, though, to learn about the imminent opening of the Thorn Centre. And especially the cricket nets.

118

"And five-a-side football, they're going to do," Kim said. "That's the thing I really envy you about being a boy. You play football at school. Much better than netball. A million times better than hockey."

David, who didn't like football, shrugged. "That's the thing I envy you about being a girl. You can say things like that."

"What d'you mean?"

"You've got that freedom. If you like football, or anything that's supposed to be mostly a boy's thing, you can just say so. Imagine a boy saying he wished he could do girls' things. You just *can't*. Girls can be any way they like. Tomboys or little ladies or anything. You can like sport, or not like sport. But when you're a boy you've got to be mad on football or there's something wrong with you."

Kim thought about this; it dawned on her that perhaps David's school life was not always as smooth and pleasant as she had assumed. "But you climb mountains," she said. "That's a much tougher thing to do. It's dangerous."

"Ah, but you're not kicking a ball, are you? So it doesn't count."

"What about cricket, though? You're ever so good at that."

"Cricket doesn't count either. Not in the same way. It's terribly second-best. The Thinking Man's Alternative. And Thinking Men just ain't tough. You're not supposed to *think*. If you *thought*, you might realize how much better a game cricket is . . ."

Kim disagreed with this; she far preferred football. Cricket was so *slow*. "I invented a new sort of cricket the other day," she said. "A livelier sort. I invented it while I was watching a bit of the Test Match. It's called Amputation Cricket." David looked interested; amputation was another of their favourite things. "You have six balls to an over, just like in ordinary cricket, only all six are bowled at the same time, by six different bowlers. It doesn't matter about keeping *wickets* intact. The winners are the side with the most *batsmen* left intact."

"Oh, that's terrific. Why amputation, though?"

"Well, all the batsmen, smashed to smithereens. Bits of batsmen flying around everywhere. Just think about it. All the cricket words. What do they call the two sides of the pitch? Leg and Off. And what about *stumps*? All it takes is a fine cut to leg . . . to slip . . . Amputation. Bring on the Extra Leg."

"That's *brilliant*. Did you really make that up all by yourself?"

"Yes. I told you."

"You are clever, you know. And talking about amputations just reminded me. You *still* haven't told me the Rat Torture!"

"So I haven't. Are you sure you wouldn't rather hear about the Grand Duchess Anastasia and the murderous Bolsheviks?"

"You mean the Romanovs? The ones that were shot in a cellar?"

"You *know* about it."

"Yes, of course. I never dreamed you didn't."

"Isn't it horrible?"

"If it happened, it's horrible. Only I don't believe it did, not any more. My mother's got this book, a newish one. There's an awful lot of evidence that it didn't happen that way at all. I'll lend it to you, if you like."

"Thanks," Kim said, somewhat hesitantly. She had never really given much thought to the possibility, briefly referred to by her father, that the massacre hadn't really happened at all. If it hadn't — well, she'd certainly have to rethink. Anastasia might still be alive! It was remotely possible. She suddenly realized that she didn't *want* Anastasia to be alive. It was so much better the other way. For Kim, the great attraction of the Tsar's children was their violent end. They were romantic, tragic figures, and that was how she wanted them to stay. She knew she would never read David's book.

"The *Rat Torture*," said David, firmly. Kim told him. They agreed that it was truly terrible. It was the worst yet. "We always say that, though. And we always manage to find something worse still."

Kim nodded. "And don't tell Anna."

"Why not?"

"I can't have my little baby sister scared," Kim said virtuously.

"Goldilocks scared? That'll be the day. She'd relish it. I wonder how she's getting on. What is this Kidsline anyway? I've never heard of it."

"Lucky you. We've been *forced* to listen, all week. It's a sort of programme within a programme. This bloke Bill Maloney does the seven to ten show on week-day mornings — it's half an hour in the middle of that. There's What's on Today — that's places to go and things to do — and a few recorded interviews, and silly little items, and the kids write in and Bill reads their letters out. They do other features, too. I expect Anna will be reading things, mostly. She always used to hate Kidsline. Now of course she's just discovered it's the most wonderful programme in the world."

"Well, if she makes it, tell me what day she's going to be on. I'd like to hear her."

"If she makes it," said Kim, "all of *Canley* will know. She'll arrange to have the programme broadcast in the streets on loudspeakers."

"You are *cruel* to her."

"Oh — do you really think so?"

"Well — not cruel." David was puzzled; that didn't sound like Kim. "You like her really. Yes you do. And she admires you like anything." Kim spluttered; David continued unperturbed. "But you'd both of you die before you'd admit it. Perhaps you don't even know it."

"Frances," Kim said, having digested these startling comments, "says we're awful to each other the whole time, and it's terrible for anyone who has to listen, and her friend Janice won't even come to our *house* any more because she can't bear it." There — now she'd get a second opinion, from someone not closely involved.

"Oh, that's daft. That's taking it too far. Of course you get at each other. I always think it's very entertaining, myself. Perhaps it's different when you have to live in the same house with the two of you. I wouldn't know."

"Do you think I ought to be — try to be nicer to her?"

"Well. Not all the time. Neither of you could stand it. *Are* you trying to?"

"Not really. I'm playing games with her. She's confused. Doesn't know if she's coming or going."

"There you are then. You *can't* be nice to her. It's not possible. It's not in your natures. But you couldn't do without each other for a moment. You'd be bored to death. You sharpen your brains on each other. Tone it down a bit if you like. But go on being yourselves. I'll tell you what I think. People like Frances and her friend — always nice, and so unexciting — think something's wrong if everyone else isn't as unexciting as they are. And think how dull the world would be then."

"Frances unexciting?" Kim wasn't certain whether to allow this, even from David.

"I'm not criticizing. It's a fact, that's all. I *like* her. But look at it this way. You and Anna enjoy yourselves like crazy, having your sort of verbal duels. That's two people out of five. Frances doesn't like it. That's one. Even if your mother and Kerry were to agree with her I still reckon you're entitled to be as beastly as you want for two-fifths of the time. Strike a happy medium. And if this Janice is so

122

easily put off, I wouldn't think she's much of a friend."

"Really? But they've always been such close friends . . ."

"Well, she ought to buck her ideas up a bit, then," David said, unsympathetically.

"You're too sensible for your own good," Kim said, sternly, and added: "Thanks."

"My pleasure. I always rather wanted to be an Agony Uncle. By the way, there's something else I meant to ask you. About Kerry. Now that your Mum's at home all day, wouldn't it be possible for her to teach Kerry at home? Then there wouldn't be any of this school bother."

"I'm not sure that's legal. And she's only going to be at home until she finds another job." Although, the way things were going, that could be a long time . . . "I suppose she might, for a while. I hope she'd have better luck than I did, that's all."

"Have you tried to teach Kerry, then? I never knew."

"I've *tried*. It's hopeless. She sits there, all sweet and innocent, and you talk for about five minutes trying to explain something, and then she says 'Oh, look, the sun's come out.' I suppose it just reminds her too much of school, that's all."

"Possibly." To David, it sounded much more as if Kerry just didn't fancy learning. But he remembered how Kim had reacted to criticism of her father; knowing that Kerry was joint top of the pops, he kept wisely silent.

10

"I WAS SITTING *here*," said Anna, "and Bill was *there*, and I had a microphone all of my own, and he said we'd do it just like it was a real live programme. And I read out What's On Today, and a letter, and we had a sort of chat. And I played a jingle on the machine! And . . ."

"Was the studio very big?"

"Oh no, it was tiny! There was a sort of a glass wall, with people behind it . . ."

"Engineers," said Kim.

"And we both had things on our heads . . ."

"Headphones."

"And afterwards he played me back a recording of the whole thing and I heard how I had talked! I thought Bill was *lovely* — he's all sort of sad and droopy with a moustache . . ."

"Sounds ravishing."

"And there's a red light that comes on and it means you're on the air. And Bill's got to work all these machines by himself! There's things that slide up and down, and he puts records on these round things . . ."

"Turntables."

"Look, it was me that went, not you! And he said it was *very good* and I could come and do the programme with him on Monday. Only Mum said I *couldn't*." Anna scowled at her mother. "She said it would have to be Tuesday instead." Twenty-four extra hours to wait! If she died during those twenty-four hours she'd *never* be on the radio and her mother would never forgive herself . . .

"I told you, Anna. I have to go somewhere else on Monday."

"Tuesdays are much better than Mondays, anyhow," Kim said.

"Why?"

"Because on Mondays everyone sleeps in later after the week-end, of course. I'm surprised you didn't think of that."

"Oh yes. *Good*." Fortunately, Anna didn't think too deeply about this statement.

"Did you meet whatshername?" asked Frances. "Bridget?"

"Yes, of course. She came to meet us in the reception place. And afterwards she took us to the canteen, and I had a strawberry milk shake."

"She was very nice," said Mrs. Tate. "I was talking to her while you were with Bill in the studio."

"What did she say?"

"You'll never know, will you? Where are all those things you brought home? The ones they gave you."

"Oh yes," said Anna. "I forgot." She went out of the room.

"You know," Kim said, "I thought she'd be a lot more worked up about it. I thought she'd be practically uncontrollable." Anna, who had lingered by the door, overheard this, and was well pleased, for this was precisely the impression she had intended to create. It was going to be her new image — the cool, calm, blasé professional. She took things like radio shows absolutely in her stride, nowadays. There was nothing to it.

"All these things they gave me," she said, returning. "Radio Thames badges. Stickers. A poster. The *Kidsline Joke Book*."

"Can I have a badge?" Kerry asked.

"Yes, of course you can. And look at this! A photograph of Bill, and he's signed it for me." This reminded Anna that she must start to practise her own signature right away.

"He does look rather droopy," Kim said, examining the photograph.

"He needs watering," said Kerry.

"He needs a facelift," said Kim. Anna glared at them. It wouldn't do. They ought to be impressed.

"I'm going to make a *list*," she said, ominously, and went off to find paper and pencil.

"Don't list me," Kim said. "I've enough problems already, without being listed."

"I won't," Anna said darkly. "And you'll be sorry." She smoothed the paper and settled down to work. Bill had promised to play a record for her, after she went off the air; she was to make a list of dedications. This was power. All the people who had offended her in the past would regret it, bitterly. Anna began to write 'Dedications' at the top of the page, but she couldn't think quite how to spell it, and gave up after the first four letters. It didn't matter. The names were the thing.

Soon she had a list of thirty-two. Now for the selection process — the elimination of those who hadn't made the grade. This was the good bit. She began to score names through, thickly and blackly, with a secret smile. Gran was first for the chop. Her fourteen friends were whittled relentlessly down to six. She couldn't decide about Kim, and put a question mark.

Only thirteen of the starters finished the course. Anna copied these names neatly on to a fresh sheet of paper, and took this upstairs to her private secret bedroom drawer.

"I wonder if she wants to keep that," said Mrs. Tate, glancing at the rough copy. "I'd better not throw it . . .oh."

"What?"

"Anna seems to be planning a massacre," said Mrs. Tate. "She's drawn up a death list, and we're all on it. I just thought you ought to know."

"She's . . ." They all went to have a look. It did seem somewhat extreme, even for Anna. But there it was. It was a most arresting document; a list of names, the majority crossed out, and at the top, in firm, large letters, the single word:

DEAD

There was something very final about this.

"It's the crossed-off names that *really* bother me," said Mrs. Tate. "According to this she's eliminated nineteen people already."

"Look," said Frances. "Kim's got a question mark. I wonder why."

"There would seem to be an element of doubt about Kim," her mother said. "Perhaps she's actually in the process of slaughtering Kim. Perhaps she's poisoned her, and she's waiting to see if it works."

"Ah," said Kim. And then — "I think you should know that I don't feel very well. Not — not well at all. Very far from well. I feel . . . very strange . . . very strange . . ."

Mrs. Tate looked around at them, impishly. Kerry gave a sudden squirm of delight, and ran out to the hall. "Anna!" she called. "Kim's dying! Come and see!" Anna arrived at full pelt to find her eldest sister writhing on the floor, while the other two stood sadly by, and her mother faintly muttered: "So young — so young . . ." Kim gave a final twitch, and was still. Mrs. Tate sighed heavily, picked up the pencil and struck her name firmly off the list.

Mrs. Tate's remark about having to go somewhere on Monday had not gone unnoticed by Kim. She thought about it; she didn't much like the sound of it. "Have you got any idea where she's going?" she asked Frances later, but Frances said: "Probably to see about selling the *furniture*," and Kim wished she'd kept her mouth shut.

She decided to keep out of the house as much as possible over the week-end. Things were pretty much all right with Frances now, but there was still a very faint after-taste from the row, and remarks like that didn't help. On Saturday morning Kim and David went swimming; in the afternoon they wrote down the rules of Amputation Cricket. On Sunday, they finally made it to Warren Hill. It was a gorgeous day. Nothing happened. Far too many things seemed to have been happening lately. Bryony was due back in the evening; David wore black. On the way home they made a slight détour and cycled past the Thorn Centre, to see how it was looking. It looked exactly as it had for the past six months, except that now a sign had been put up: Opening 4th September. The sign had been defaced by vandals. All the Tates were very interested in the Centre, not least Anna, who had long been aware that the Duke who was coming to open it had a son just two years older than herself.

During the evening Kim watched her mother closely, searching for clues in her behaviour, but learned nothing, except that it couldn't be anything *very* disastrous, for Mrs. Tate was cheerful enough, if a little jittery. Dentist? No, she'd have said. Could she be going to see their father? Why should that be a secret, though? She dressed very smartly on Monday morning, and departed at half past nine, still giving them not a hint, just: "I shan't be very long." Which seemed to rule out Dad. Or did it? Kim gave up. She went to find Kerry.

Kerry was in her bedroom, building. She was being creative with the Lego. Kim, looking at the result, wondered if this might be the architectural equivalent of abstract art.

"I like the wheels on the roof. Very original."

"We should have more wheels," said Kerry. "I like wheels. What are you frowning about?"

"Just wondering where Mum can have gone. She hasn't told *anybody*."

"I expect she's gone to get a job," Kerry said. "Look, there's another set of wheels by your foot. I thought I was one short."

Mrs. Tate was gone just under two hours. She walked in, doleful and dejected; she looked around at her assembled daughters, threw her handbag on to a chair, broke into a gleeful grin and whooped.

"Well, you lot. I've got a job! Let's have a celebration. It's at least a fortnight since the last one."

"*Teasing* us!" Kim said indignantly.

Her mother smiled wickedly. "Don't you want to know?"

"Of course!"

"Well — it's at the Thorn Centre. Apart from the sports facilities, you see, there's also a restaurant, and a bar — no, I'm not going to be a barmaid, Frances — and a sports shop. And I happened to see an advertisement for someone to manage the sports shop, in that pink newsletter Kim brought."

"You're going to be manageress of a sports shop?"

"Sounds like it."

"Tennis rackets and things?"

"Tennis rackets, squash rackets, training shoes, shuttlecocks, track suits — you name it, I'll be selling it."

"Track suits?" Kim had pined for a track suit, for ages. "Will you get discount?"

"Certainly I will. I should think a track suit might be very possible by Christmas. And — wait for *this* — all of us are entitled to free membership! We can use the Centre as much as we like without paying a penny. Isn't that good?"

"That is fantastic." Fantastic wasn't nearly enough of a word, but Kim could think of nothing better, on the spur of the moment. Unlimited free access to all those sports — and a very possible track suit . . .

"I don't understand, though," said Frances. "Why didn't they advertise in the Gazette?"

"Ah, well, they *did*, you see. A few weeks ago; at the same time as they were having the booklet printed, more or less. They couldn't get anybody. Perhaps most of the job-seekers *are* school leavers. I've been incredibly lucky. I don't know a thing about sports equipment; in a strong field I wouldn't have stood an earthly. As it was, Mr. Truman — he's the man who interviewed me, he runs the Centre — he was very glad to take me with the experience I *have* got. See how anxious he was? He interviewed me as soon as was humanly possible — first thing Monday morning."

"Is the money as good as you were getting at Wilshires?" Frances asked.

"Better," said her mother. "Much, much better. We needn't worry now for a while. No bus fares either — I can walk it in ten minutes. It seems almost too good to be true. Mr. Wilshire did me a real favour. I knew it would turn out for the best."

"So — you'll be starting work when the Centre opens, in September?"

"Oh, before that! There's masses to be done before the public come in. I thought I'd go along some time this week — Wednesday, perhaps — and have a look. Mr. Truman suggested that I should. You can all come along, if you like. Have a sneak preview."

Anna wasn't sure about all this. She was *pleased* that her mother had found a job. At least, she thought she was — she hadn't actually got around to weighing up the pros and

130

cons, yet. But it was rather mean of her to have found it on the very day before Anna's radio debut. She felt that her thunder was being stolen.

"Do you know," Kim was saying, "Kerry guessed where you'd gone. She was the only one who did. But why didn't you tell us?"

"Is that true, Kerry? How did you know?"

"I didn't know. It just seemed the most likely thing. I took it for granted that was what you'd gone to do."

"You're a clever girl. Oh, Kim, I just didn't want to raise any false hopes. If I hadn't got the job I'd probably never have told you a thing about it."

"You're the clever one," Kim said. "It's the best job you could possibly have got. You're brilliant."

"Well, thanks — and weren't we going to celebrate? Right. We'll go to the cinema. This afternoon. The new Disney's on at Thornton Cross. I'll check the times, in the paper . . ."

Anna thought not. An outing was going too far. This job business was beginning to assume ridiculous proportions; at this rate tomorrow would be a positive anticlimax. She'd have no thunder left to steal. After about half an hour, she began to look wan. She became very quiet. She sidled up to her mother and said:

"We won't be able to go out, I don't think. I feel very sick."

"Oh, darling, I am sorry. I expect you're nervous about tomorrow. But I'm sure you wouldn't want us all to stay home just because of that. I'll ring Gran and ask her to come round and sit with you. How's that?" The sickness passed off; Anna decided that she would, after all, be well enough to go. But her mother was anxious that nothing should set the sickness off again; while the others guzzled chocolate ripple ice cream, popcorn and hot dogs, Anna had to be content with barley sugar, which is so very good for a queasy stomach.

"I thought she did very well." David had come to the Tates' house to share with Anna's sisters the experience of listening to Anna's debut. Or, as Kim put it, to sustain them through their darkest half-hour.

"Hang on," said Frances. "There's half a minute to go yet."

"And so," said Bill Maloney, "with the news at the top of the hour approaching fast, it's time to say a great big thank you to our guest presenter on today's Kidsline, Anna Tate. Have you had a good time, Anna?"

"Yes, thanks, Bill. I've had a marvellous time."

"A very unusual young lady, and I'm sure we're going to hear a lot more of her. In the next half hour of the show I'll be playing a record for Anna and all her friends — she's given me a list to read out — so stay tuned, folks, you might be on it!"

Kim gave a quick writhe — she'd rather enjoyed writhing — and clutched her stomach. David chuckled. He had been much flattered to know that he was on Anna's Death List, which had been preserved for posterity. Anna, fortunately, had found the whole thing very funny, and had taken to writing In Memoriam verses to her twenty victims.

In the studio, Bill shook Anna's hand, thanked her, and told her she'd been simply wonderful. He hoped he'd see her again, one day. Anna would have liked this remark better without the 'one day'. The news ended; Bill put a Beatles oldie on — and suddenly it was over, and she had to go, because there was another guest coming in, and she was in the way. Reluctantly, she slipped out of the studio. Her mother was waiting.

"Well done, darling. I thought you were very good. Did you enjoy it?"

"*Yes.*" Why make it sound so final? Surely they were

132

going to ask her to become a regular presenter? Where was Bridget?

"She had to go to a meeting, darling. Well — are we ready to go, now?"

Bridget had gone to a *meeting*? But . . . and then she realized that this was, in fact, a very good thing. Bridget would certainly have been here to say goodbye, and well done, if it had been a final farewell. Obviously she was expecting to be seeing Anna again quite soon. She would probably ring up later today.

Anna had no doubts now. Until she broke into television, which was certain to happen, sooner or later, this was what she wanted to be. A Radio Star. And to think that she had once imagined that the world began and ended at the Josephine Priestley School! All those children trooping along to auditions, perhaps making it into a grotty little commercial; all of them having to be trained to do the things which to Anna came naturally! In a commercial you were just an anonymous face. She had a *name*. She was known to the people of London. And she'd done it all by herself! No Josephine Priestley to help her along. No connections; no famous and influential relatives pulling strings. Oh no. Anna had long envied, and bitterly resented, those offspring of well-known personalities whose pictures appeared in the papers for no other reason than the accident of their birth. Famous from the start. It was so unfair! Was it Anna's fault that neither of her parents was a celebrity? Well, now she'd show them.

It would be glorious. She had already begun to compose her own jingles — and her name was absolutely tailor-made for jingles! Everything rhymed with Tate. "It's half past eight — it's Anna Tate! Ain't that great! Just can't wait! Make a date with Anna Tate!" It was, definitely, meant. She thought perhaps she'd come to be known as the First Lady of London. And what would the people at school say? She had prudently laid in a stock of Radio Thames goodies to be distributed on the first day of term. It would all be so marvellous! If only Bridget would hurry up and ring!

Mrs. Tate, guessing that Anna would feel rather let down when it was all over — anticlimaxitis, she called it — had decided to take her out for lunch to the Tennessee Pancake House, which was Anna's favourite place. But Anna would have none of it; they must go home straight away! They mustn't delay for one single second! Since it had taken a great deal of effort on her part actually to prise Anna out of the Radio Thames building, Mrs. Tate was understandably confused. But she didn't argue; this was Anna's day, and they would do as Anna wished. They hurried home as if their lives depended on it.

"What was it like?" Frances was in the hall, waiting for them.

"It was fine," said Anna. "Has the phone rung?" Mrs. Tate began to understand.

"No. Oh, come on. Tell us." And Anna told them; she relived every second, in minute detail. No, of course she hadn't been nervous. (Calm. Blasé. Professional.) It was nothing to get worked up about. She could do it *every day*. Mrs. Tate looked gloomy.

It was just before midday when the phone rang. Kim got there first.

"Call for you, Anna."

"Anna? Hello, dear. I just had to ring up and congratulate you. I was so proud! I thought you were wonderful. I told Mrs. Bates next door, and she listened too . . ."

Anna endured three minutes of this. Then she said firmly: "Gran, I really have to go now. I'm expecting a very urgent call." She couldn't have relations blocking up the line!

"That was a quick conversation, Anna," said her mother.

"It wasn't important." Twenty minutes later the phone rang again. This time Anna was ready for it, and pounced.

134

"Hello, Anna! I . . . "

"*Dad.*" Oh, this was too bad. Two disappointments in less than half an hour! Dispiritedly, she listened while her father praised her performance. Why were people so thoughtless?

"*Don't* hang up," said Mrs. Tate. "I want a word with him." She took the phone and proceeded to tell her husband about her new job, concealing the fact that she had lost her last one a fortnight before. Anna stood menacingly, accusingly, nearby, making hurry-up signals and tapping her foot.

"He got the impression you were trying to get rid of him," her mother said, hanging up. "I wonder why."

The next call came through at half past one; it was Anna's friend Annette, who had heard the show, and wanted to talk to Anna . . . The phone kept ringing, and Anna's face grew longer and longer. She spoke to Annette and to Lucy; she was reasonably civil to Tracy and Emily. But Katie was the last straw. For the first time Anna began to see that there might be disadvantages in having fourteen friends. This would have to stop. Bridget had probably been trying to get through all afternoon, and getting engaged, engaged, engaged . . . she might give up!

"I'm not talking to *anybody else*," she said. "Tell them I'm out and get rid of them as quickly as you can."

"Anna, I'll do nothing of the sort. If people are nice enough to ring up and congratulate you, you'll talk to them."

"Then I will go out! I'll really be out!" But no — of course, she couldn't go out because she had to be here to talk to Bridget! Oh, it was a nuisance. Why was everybody being so mean?

There were eleven phone calls, in all, for Anna that day. None of the callers was Bridget.

"This is ridiculous," said their mother, coming downstairs at a quarter past ten. "I just looked in on her and she's still awake. Brooding."

Frances switched off the television. "You can *feel* it, all through the house, when Anna broods."

"Excuse me if I'm being very stupid," said Kim. "But surely Kidsline is only on during the school holidays. It'll finish at the end of August."

"I wish it would. But apparently not; during the school term there's something called Saturday Kidsline instead. That's what she's got her eye on. She seems to be planning to take it over."

"But surely she's just making all this up? It *was* only a one-off, wasn't it? Nothing was ever said about her doing more than just that one programme?"

"Nothing's been said. Unless Anna knows something I don't, which is very unlikely. She keeps telling me that Bill said something to her about seeing her again. I hope to God that she hasn't built that one remark up into all this. Because I'm sure it was just a friendly sort of way of saying goodbye, that's all. And she's going to be *so* disappointed . . ."

"Oh, heck." Kim went upstairs and slipped into Anna's and Kerry's bedroom. The night light was on; Kerry was curled into a tight, sleeping ball; Anna lay on her back, gazing mournfully at the ceiling. She glanced at Kim, but said nothing.

So many things had been said to Kim about herself and Anna lately. She'd been told that she liked Anna; that Anna admired her; that they were very much alike, really; that they couldn't do without each other for a moment. Well. Let them believe what they would. Of course, the truth was that she would happily strangle the little monster at the drop of a hat.

"Look," she said gently, perching on the end of Anna's bed. "She couldn't possibly have rung today, you know."

"Why not?"

136

"Because she'd have to arrange it with all sorts of other people first. You can't take somebody on as a regular presenter, just like that. It's a big decision. She'd probably have to ask the head of the station before she could do it. So even if you do hear, it won't be straight away."

"I'll hear. Perhaps tomorrow, then." You couldn't shake her. "Kim? Why are you being so nice to me?"

"God knows. Maybe because you look so pathetic lying there like a piece of chewed string."

Chewed . . ."Kim? Will you do something for me?"

"I doubt it."

"Tell me the Rat Torture!"

"Yes," said Kim. "All right. I will. First of all, you need a rat. You give the rat a huge meal. Then you tie the victim down on his back, and you put the rat on to his bare stomach."

"Ooooh." Anna's eyes were huge and round.

"Then you place a transparent lid over the rat. Quite a big one. The lid has air holes so the rat can breathe. Then you wait. And eventually the rat will get hungry again. And the only thing for it to eat is the victim. So he's lying there, watching — you prop his head up so he gets a good view — and, slowly, bit by bit, the rat begins to eat down into his stomach . . ."

"Ooooh!" Anna squirmed, feeling sharp wicked teeth tearing at her flesh. "Kim, that's horrible!"

"Hush. You'll wake Kerry."

"But why do you give the rat a meal first? That's silly. You have to wait so much longer for it to get hungry and start . . .eating . . ."

"Really, Anna, you've no idea about torture, have you? Don't they teach you anything at school? Torture is *slow*. The victim has to lie there for ages, watching and waiting and imagining . . . you never rush a good torture. The victim would like to get it over with as soon as possible. So you string it out. That's how it works."

"I see." She would remember that. It would be very useful to know. "Tell me another one, Kim."

"No more tortures. You ought to be asleep."

"Please?"

"Well — I'll tell you a story."

"Oh no. That's dull."

"Not this one isn't. It's even worse than the Rat Torture." Well — it was taking her mind off Kidsline, at any rate. "Once upon a time, there were four sisters. The youngest one was called the Grand Duchess Anastasia . . ."

That night, Anna had her first nightmare.

"You can't blame me," Kim said. "I thought she was enjoying it. I was trying to cheer her up."

"*I did enjoy it,*" Anna said, rather hollowly. They were at breakfast. "I did!"

"What on earth were you telling her?" asked Mrs Tate.

"Just things," Kim said vaguely. "A bedtime story."

"I guessed why you had to feed the rat first," Kerry said, cutting her toast in half, diagonally.

"You — but you were asleep!"

"That," said her mother, "clearly qualifies as one of the stupidest remarks of the week. What is all this, anyway? Funeral Directors. In Memoriam. Now rats. I don't know. You're all warped."

"It was only a torture," said Kerry. "I liked it."

"There you are! It gets worse! Warped."

"I'm not warped," Frances said. "I don't want to know about rats and torture. Or funerals."

Unexciting, thought Kim, and winced. Her own sister.

"I'm glad to hear it," said Mrs Tate. "Now, who wants to come along to the Thorn Centre with me? A bit of fresh air will do you all good. Unwarp you a bit. I've rung Mr. Truman — he's expecting us." Kim and Kerry agreed at once, but Anna would not be budged. The telephone might ring, and she must be here to answer it.

"Anna, I really think you should come out for a while. You can't wait in indefinitely. We'll only be gone a couple of hours."

"No," said Anna.

"I'll stay with her," said Frances, who strongly suspected that Kim had upset Anna deliberately, though Anna firmly denied this, which was surprising. So Anna waited in. She waited in all day, and Bridget didn't ring. By the evening, Anna was looking just slightly more animated than a corpse, and even Frances was wishing with all her heart that Kidsline had never been invented.

11

KERRY HAD BEEN VERY unexpected, lately. She kept surprising Kim in small but significant ways. For so long, now, Kerry had seemed almost exactly the same. Perhaps she was finally starting to develop new sides and depths that Kim didn't know about. But then, she was always so quiet that it was all but impossible to guess at what went on inside her head. To think that *Anna* had had the nightmare, while Kerry listened happily to the whole gory thing and slept untroubled. Kim could have sworn it would be the other way around. Perhaps she didn't know them, either of them, as well as she'd thought she did . . . And Kerry noticed, and she remembered. That was another thing. Kim had mentioned to her about wondering if she would manage to say twenty words, while they had been at Mrs. Hanrahan's. Kerry was silent for a while; then, when Kim had forgotten all about it, she said: "Thirty-four."

"What?"

"Thirty-four words I said altogether."

"How do you know? You can't possibly. It was six *days* ago."

"I just counted them. Thirty-four."

"You remember — word for word? It's not possible."

"But I do," said Kerry, and promptly began to repeat the

entire conversation."You said: 'My sister's a secret coffee drinker and I've only just found it out.' Then Mrs. Hanrahan said to me: 'I can see we're going to . . . ' "

"All right," Kim said after a minute or so. "I believe you." It was rather eerie. What other tricks could Kerry do? A human tape recorder. It might come in very useful, some day.

Kim returned from her morning walk on Thursday full of apprehension. She had never believed that Bridget would ring. It was all a mad dream. But how did you say that to Anna? And why couldn't Anna be contented with just one radio appearance? It was more than most people ever did. And now, with each hour that passed, Anna was sinking lower and lower, and the spirits of her whole family were automatically sinking too. It was so *stupid*. Just when things were starting to go well — her mother had a job, the book was nearly finished — but, of course, to Anna these things mattered not one jot. The next few days would be grim. Kim opened the front door, and braced herself to face the blast of depression.

"Kim? Is that Kim? Come and see!" No. Oh no. It wasn't possible.

"Look! They wrote to me!" Anna — a miraculously revitalized Anna, a glowing and dancing Anna — thrust a sheet of paper into her hand. "Read it!" Kim looked at the letter with incredulity. Anna was a witch. She had done magic. She had hypnotized the entire staff of Radio Thames. There was no other way. "Read it!"

"All *right*." She read:

Dear Anna,

Many congratulations on your successful appearance on Kidsline. The experiment of inviting young listeners to be guest presenters has been so well received that, after much discussion, we have decided to extend the idea. As

141

you know, during the school term Kidsline moves to a two-hour slot on Saturday mornings. We plan to have four children — working on a rota basis — to co-present the programme with the regular disc jockey. If you would be interested in doing this, please ask your mother to give me a ring. Do think it over properly; we don't want people who are going to tire of it and drop out after a couple of shows.

Yours sincerely,
BRIDGET MUNROE.

"You see?" said Anna, hopping up and down. "You were right, Kim. Look what she wrote: 'after much discussion we have decided'. She *did* have to go and talk it over with the head of Radio Thames. That's why it's taken so long."

It didn't seem very long to Kim — Bridget had written on the day following Anna's show — but she didn't argue. If Anna wanted to interpret her comforting platitudes as words of great wisdom, then that was fine by her. "I know everything," she said. "I've always told you that." But how could Anna have known? Kim would have given odds of a million to one against this happening.

"I *knew*," said Anna. "I knew they'd ask me." That was just it. She'd never doubted. Perhaps if you believed in yourself as strongly as that, it could actually work miracles. Kim resolved to try it some time.

"When are you going to ring, Mum?"

"I've rung already," said her mother. "I rang within twenty seconds of Anna reading the letter. Do you think I had any choice?"

"Think it over," Anna said scornfully. "I didn't have to think it over. I *have* thought." Nobody could deny that.

"She's going to be paid," said her mother. "Twenty pounds a time. It's ridiculous. I have to work the best part of a day to earn twenty pounds."

Anna hadn't realized that she would actually be paid to do Kidsline, but she had successfully concealed the fact. It wouldn't do to be surprised. She was a professional; naturally she would be paid.

"I talked to Bridget on the phone," she said. "This is what's going to happen. I'll be on every other Saturday, with some boy, and another boy and girl will do the Saturdays in between. Of course I'll be much the youngest because they won't *consider* anyone under nine except me." She would win the hearts of all the listeners. She would captivate London. She would steal the show.

"Who does Saturday Kidsline? Bill?"

"No, he doesn't work Saturdays. It's somebody called Chris Devonshire. But I expect he'll be just as nice. I hope he's got a moustache too." Anna was very taken with the moustache.

"Loyal, aren't you? I thought Bill was so *lovely*." Kim had heard Chris Devonshire once or twice, and thought the moustache unlikely, since she was a woman. She decided not to enlighten Anna. "Well," she said sadly, "I suppose we'll have to get used to some changes, now. We'll have to go ex-directory, of course — and put barbed wire up to stop Anna's fans leaping into the garden and hurling themselves against the window . . ."

Anna looked enchanted at the prospect.

Kim didn't expect to be paid that Thursday evening. McCluskey's owners were returning in a few days' time, and surely it would make more sense to pay her on her last day of employment. But no — Mrs. Hanrahan was there at the door, and asked her in. Kim had to admit that their conversations had, so far, been greatly to her advantage; she'd been able to reassure Frances about next term, and she'd discovered Mr. Hanrahan's superb profession — and, of course, she'd heard the news of the Thorn Centre. She

143

told Mrs. Hanrahan about her mother's new job. It all helped to delay the fateful moment when she had to drink the coffee.

"That's good news. By the way, I made a point of listening to your young sister on the radio. Very self-assured for seven, isn't she?"

"That's one way of putting it, yes. Well, they must have liked her, because they've asked her to do a show once a fortnight, starting in September. I just hope it's not going to turn her head altogether."

"That's what elder sisters are for," said Mrs. Hanrahan. "To see that heads remain unturned." Kim nodded: very true, very true. "Now, here's your pay. John and Rosemary are collecting the hound on Monday — hear that, McCluskey? Mother's coming to get you." McCluskey yawned. "So I'll give you your final three days' pay on Sunday evening. All right?"

"Yes, that's fine. I've really rather enjoyed it. It'll seem strange at first, when he's gone."

"Ah. I'm glad you said that. You see, the peril of having a son working for an airline is that he can take off so frequently and so cheaply. They've decided to spend Christmas on St. Lucia. So . . ."

"Yes," said Kim. "Of course I will." Lovely extra Christmas money. Good.

"I'll let you know further details at a later date. Well. How's Kerry?"

"She's O.K. Look — she's really sorry about that bottle. So am I."

"There's no need to keep apologizing for what was obviously an accident."

"And she's always very quiet, you know. I mean, she wasn't being rude or anything."

"It never crossed my mind that she might be. Kim — will you answer me one question?"

144

"Er — yes, of course." What now?

"Do you know if anybody in your family had difficulty in learning to read?"

"I don't think so . . . no, wait. My uncle Jack did. He still couldn't read when he was eleven, Mum said. And my great-grandmother was the same. But there's nothing wrong with them," she said hastily. How had Mrs. Hanrahan known? "They were late developers, you see."

"Ah," said Mrs. Hanrahan. And suddenly Kim thought — she knows! She knows something about Kerry, and she's going to tell me now — after all this time — and I'm not prepared! I'm not ready for it!

"You know," said Mrs. Hanrahan, "I wonder if you haven't been looking at this back to front. You've assumed, right, that Kerry can't read or write because she's hardly been to school. I think it's the other way round."

"She hasn't been to school . . . because she can't read . . . but that doesn't make sense." What *was* this?

Mrs. Hanrahan said simply: "I'm almost certain that Kerry's dyslexic."

"She's . . ." No! There was nothing wrong with Kerry! All the old ghosts poked their fearsome, taunting heads out from the cobwebs. Backward . . . subnormal . . . no!

"Have you ever *heard* of dyslexia?"

"Dyslexia rules K.O.," Kim said, automatically. There! It was something that people wrote mocking RULES O.K. graffiti about!

"I beg your pardon?"

"Oh, it's just something written on the wall by the park. It's a RULES O.K. joke. Dyslexia rules K.O. I never understood it."

"Oh, I see. The letters the wrong way round. Dyslexics often reverse letter order when they write . . . look, let me explain."

"I don't think I want to know."

145

"Kim, for goodness sake act your age. Do you want to help Kerry or don't you? Just say the word and I'll go over your head and telephone your mother."

There was no doubt, then. She was that certain. "All right. I'm sorry. Go on."

" 'Dyslexic' is a word used to describe people who, although they may be perfectly intelligent in other ways, find it terribly difficult to learn to read, write or spell."

Kim's head buzzed. "No! It can't be that. There's nothing like that wrong with Kerry — she's *got* to learn to read. She's not going to grow up to be — what is it? — illiterate. That's awful! It's beginning to be awkward already and she's only eight!"

"I didn't say she wouldn't learn, Kim. She can learn. But she has to be prepared to work, work, work at it. Dyslexic children can be given special teaching nowadays. She'll have every chance. Your uncle Jack can read, can't he? And he was almost certainly dyslexic too. It often runs in families. Kerry will learn. She's just got to be persuaded to try. I promise you, she'll learn. And it's nothing to be ashamed of! It's quite common, in one degree or another. It's not a stigma, or a handicap, or a disability. Just a rather awkward little problem. That's all."

Nobody, but nobody, ever used that tone of voice about something they didn't know from personal experience. Kim hesitated, then said: "Mrs. Hanrahan — your son had dyslexia, didn't he?"

"John? Oh, no. Me."

"*You?* You were dyslexic?"

"Am, not was. It doesn't go away. And, as you see, I am neither backward nor illiterate."

"No, I know." Kim was flustered, and confused. "I didn't mean that you were . . . But I just don't understand. How is it possible to be normally — *more* than normally intelligent — and not be able to read?"

146

"Well, that's the mystery. I've never gone into it too deeply. I did read something about hemispheres of the brain, and that was enough for me. When it's *your* hemispheres they're talking about . . . anyway, I can tell you what it feels like. It feels as if your head is jammed up and you can't unjam it. It's very frustrating."

"Is this why you wanted to meet Kerry? Did you guess — from something I said?"

"The moment you told me that she was eight, and bright, and couldn't read or write, my ears pricked up. As I told you, there are different sorts of dyslexia. Not everyone shows the same symptoms. But Kerry seems very much as I was. Poor co-ordination — that's what causes the trips and stumbles and breakages."

"It was true, then, when you told her you broke things too — and I thought you were just comforting her."

"Absolutely true. I was the most un-coordinated child. I'll try to explain what it was like, learning to read. In the first place, I couldn't recognize all the letters of the alphabet. P, b, d, q, even g, they all looked so horribly alike. And I was for ever writing letters the wrong way round. Take 'r'. Can you picture an 'r'? Of course you can. Well, I couldn't. I couldn't remember what it looked like. And it was no use trying to remember that the vertical line was on the left, because I used to confuse left and right. It was the same for all the other letters. And then there were the capitals, just to make things worse. And even if I knew the letters, how to make any sense out of words? They never looked like words. They were groups of letters with spaces in between. Take a word — any word. Choose one."

"Um — coffee."

"Right. Now, you can see quite clearly in your mind what the word 'coffee' looks like. And if you'd just come across it for the first time, you'd recognize it the next time you saw it. That's what dyslexic children can't do. Every time I met 'coffee' I had to work it out all over again. Just another confusing jumble of letters to be decoded into a word. You see why it's so difficult to learn to read? And writing! If you can't remember what 'coffee' looks like, how are you to know how to spell it? You try and do it phonetically. And imagine how that turns out, with a treacherous language like English. You might try 'cofe' and it would look just as good as it does the other way. I used to think I was fearfully stupid. The teachers thought I was lazy."

"Kerry thinks she's stupid," Kim said slowly. It was like the last chapter of a detective story; all the clues were suddenly fitting together, as the detective revealed the solution, the solution that should have been obvious all along, only everyone but the detective was too dumb to see it. "Mrs. Hanrahan — you read all right now. What happened?"

"I just worked, that's all. I was *determined* to read. And don't believe it's easy, even now. I still have my days. Days when — well, my head jams. I wake with a blinding headache, and I just keep myself out of circulation for the day, because I know that my brain won't work properly, and I'll make the most ridiculous mistakes. But most of the time I manage. It's just that I have to make a conscious effort to do what most people do without even thinking about it."

"Nobody would ever know," Kim said, with sincere admiration.

"Good. That's the idea."

"Don't they — the other teachers — don't any of them know?"

"Nobody at school knows. And I'm sure you won't be telling them, will you? It's a sort of pride, really. As long as nobody realizes, then I've beaten it. I've won. I'm a past master at not letting people know. You learn all sorts of tricks. Even when I was a child — the things I thought up, to hide the fact that I could hardly read — to get by at

148

school. Losing my voice was my favourite. I used to practise. I can still do it. Listen." She spoke a few words, hoarse, rasping, barely audible. It sounded agonizing. "So I could get out of reading aloud, you see? *And* I was allowed to suck throat lozenges in class . . . the others thought it terribly unfair. And I was short-sighted, so when we went out I'd leave my glasses behind. Nobody could expect me to read what I couldn't see, could they?"

"But how did you manage your school work? How could you learn enough to pass exams, if you couldn't read? Didn't anybody know that you were dyslexic?"

"I never even heard the word until I was twenty, at least. I got by, on the whole, by paying very close attention in class. Listening. Mostly people didn't bother too much — they knew it was all written down in the text-books. But I listened to every word. I could read, after a fashion, by the time I was eleven or twelve, but it was a painfully slow process. More like deciphering than reading. I survived, thanks to intelligence, quick wits and considerable cunning. And a gift for mathematics; I never had much trouble with numbers. I developed a very good memory for the spoken word, to compensate for the visual memory that let me down so badly."

"Kerry's got that already! She remembers every book I read her — even if she's only heard it once. And she can repeat conversations *exactly* — word for word. Look — I do see that she must have dyslexia. But would it cause all this? Do most dyslexic children get school phobia? Did you?"

"No — but it wasn't exactly my favourite place, as you can imagine. Kerry's reaction does seem rather extreme, but I think I understand. She's a clever child. Think, for a moment, how she must have felt. She began to realize that she *couldn't* grasp even the basics of reading and writing. All her friends were galloping ahead, and she wasn't even crawling. And — here I'm guessing — her teacher might say: 'Now, Kerry, that's just stupid. You knew it a minute ago.' And she'd think: 'But I did know it a minute ago! So why don't I know it now? If the others can do it, why can't I? What's wrong with me?' She knew she was clumsy and awkward. And so she began to believe . . .'"

"That she was retarded! But I guessed that. I just never realized that she had any real reason to think it. She never told me — not anything . . ." This hurt.

"No wonder she didn't want to go to school. If she hadn't been so intelligent it probably wouldn't have happened. The frustration of it. The *fear* — every single day. I know how she felt. I remember how she felt. It was just that her reaction was different. It came to be more of a horror than she could bear. It literally made her sick."

For the first time, Kim realized what people meant when they said 'it was like a great weight being lifted from my shoulders'. It *was* like that. You were so used to the weight that you hardly knew it was there any more. And then, suddenly, it was gone. Because there was no doubt. Mrs. Hanrahan was absolutely right, and the mystery was solved.

"When she understands that she's in no way backward — that dyslexia is quite common, actually — I'm sure she'll be willing to work like mad to make up for all she's lost. She seemed that sort of a child. And everyone will help her."

"But will she understand it? 'Dyslexia' won't mean a thing to her. And she's so used to resisting tests and things — I don't know. I don't know if it'll get through to her, that it's different now."

"Do you think it might help if I were to try and explain it to her? I can explain it from the *inside*, you see. I ought to be able to make her understand. I think I can."

"Would you really? Yes, I think that would help a lot." And, all of a sudden, Kim wanted to do all the lunatic things that people in musicals do when something marvellous

150

happens; she wanted to leap on to the table, to dance, to sing a loud and pointless song. But Mrs. Hanrahan mightn't know the words, so she just said "Thank you."

"Wonderful woman," said Mrs. Tate, to Kim. They were riding home on the bus from Thornton Cross; Mrs. Tate had had an appointment with the education people, Kim had been shopping, battling through the queues in Sainsbury's. "How in the world can we ever thank her?"

"I don't think she wants to be thanked." Neither of them quite believed it, yet.

"Whatever she said to Kerry . . . well, it made an impression. An enormous impression. It's almost as if she thinks it's an honour to be dyslexic, if Mrs. Hanrahan is." These two were now firm friends, which put Kim in a not altogether comfortable position — her form teacher and her little sister, yakking away together . . . "And haven't you noticed a change in her? I know it's little more than a week. But she *is* changed."

"She's getting some confidence in herself," Kim said. "That was what was always missing. She's not so quiet now — not quite. She's talking more. You know, I think the reason she always said so little was that she was afraid of giving herself away. Because she thought she was so stupid and slow."

"The poor little thing. All these years . . . what she must have been going through."

"And now it's over. I haven't quite grasped that yet. Really truly over. Perhaps when I see her actually going to school, then it'll seem real. I think she's already starting to stand up to Anna more, Mum. That's got to be good. She's always let Anna walk all over her. It used to drive me spare."

"Yes, I know. Of course, the very fact of Anna being so quick, her younger sister learning to read so effortlessly — that must have made it so much worse for her. Oh, if only

151

we'd found out earlier, Kim! I'll never forgive myself for not seeing it. I *knew* about dyslexia. I *should* have guessed . . ."

"Don't you go blaming youself. The experts are the ones who should have guessed. That's what they're there for. Her teachers — why didn't they spot it? And all those psychologists. With their crackpot theories. If they'd only put two and two together instead of all that drawing pictures rubbish . . ."

"Kim, I really don't think that's fair. Apparently it's not always easy to spot dyslexia. And she never gave them a chance, did she? If she'd stuck it out at school — but she was so seldom there, after the first year, and when she *was* there they were probably too busy watching for her to start being sick . . . and as for the psychologists, they did their best to test her, didn't they? She wouldn't have it."

"And they thought she was trying to pretend that she wasn't clever! What she *was* doing was jiggering up all the tests to hide the fact that she was *stupid*." Oh, why hadn't Kim guessed? She should have found out about dyslexia. She should have worked it out somehow. She could have saved Kerry so much suffering. It was all very well, telling her mother not to blame herself. You couldn't help blaming yourself.

"And all the tests that she didn't know how to jigger up she refused to do. It's all so obvious, isn't it, when you know the reason? Well — I just hope she's going to be all right now, at school. She seems happier about it — oh, I'm sure she'll be O.K."

"She's very nervous. And I don't suppose she'll settle straight away. But she's promised Mrs. Hanrahan all sorts of things."

"Yes, I know. I suppose, really, it'll be like starting from scratch again. She's got so much catching up to do."

"She's promised Mrs. Hanrahan," Kim said again. She would have liked it a lot better if Kerry had promised *her*.

All the same — "She's really keen to learn. She *wants* to. That's what matters, isn't it? It's like a whole new world's been opened up for her. Well, I'm going to help her." Mrs. Hanrahan might be the dyslexia expert, but she didn't have a monopoly of the subject. "I'm going to read books and try and understand about dyslexia."

"You're a smasher. And they told me today that they're arranging for her to attend a special unit every week, where they have teachers trained specifically to help dyslexic children. She'll learn like wildfire."

Rain pattered against the window; it was getting ready for August Bank Holiday. Kim said suddenly: "Have you told Dad?"

"I wrote to him yesterday. There seemed to be such a lot to say — it was easier to write it down than to phone. And I asked after the book. I've been wondering if I haven't been rather — unkind — I didn't have faith — not showing any interest. It is quite an achievement."

"*Brains*," said Kim.

"Brains?"

"They're so ridiculous. Just a bit of stuff in your skull — just flesh and blood — and they're responsible for everything! I've seen a brain. It doesn't look anything much. Just something you might buy from a butcher. And yet it can learn and remember and think and calculate."

"You do buy them from the butcher. Sheep's brains."

"*You* might. I don't fancy it. You'd be eating the sheep's memory as well."

"Er — yes."

"So what is it about Kerry's brain that makes her dyslexic? And how come Dad's brain makes him so much cleverer than anybody else? What *is* it? I bet it *looks* like just another brain."

"You *are* your brain, aren't you?" Mrs. Tate fell silent.

"Mum? Are you O.K.?"

"Oh yes, I'm O.K. It's just that — thinking about brains — there's something that I've always wondered if I should tell you. It's been on my mind for years, but the time's never seemed right, somehow. Kim — promise you won't get mad at me? You'll understand that I was acting for the best, or what I thought was the best, and I still do think so, only . . ."

"Mum, cut the cackle and get on with it *please*! Of course I won't get mad at you. It sounds fascinating."

"Yes — well. Do you know about IQ tests?"

"Yes — they're how they measure intelligence."

"That's right. 100 is average. Anything over 150 is supposed to put you in the genius range. Well, your father's got an IQ of a hundred and fifty something. I can't remember exactly."

"So he's a real proper genius? My own father?"

"Technically. I think it's a completely meaningless term, myself."

"No wonder he used to spend so much time on his own solving puzzles," was Kim's rather surprising first reaction to this news. "None of us could ever keep up with him. But you couldn't expect us to, could you? I suppose when you're a genius — well, it must sometimes be sort of dull, living with a houseful of ordinary people."

"Well, that's what I'm trying to explain. He wasn't."

"Sorry, I've lost you."

"He wasn't living with a houseful of ordinary people — if by 'ordinary' you mean non-genius, which I certainly wouldn't accept for a moment. Everybody is extraordinary, in their own way. Brains aren't everything . . . Kim, they gave you an IQ test at school. And your IQ is two points higher than your father's."

"But — what d'you mean? I'm not a genius! It must have been wrong."

"It wasn't wrong. You've got an astounding brain, when

154

you choose to use it. And I told you 'genius' was a meaningless term."

"But I don't remember any IQ test."

"You were only five or six. Look — I've had this on my conscience, ever since then."

"Me having an IQ test?" This was nonsense. Her mother looked so worried — so guilty. And Kim most definitely wasn't a genius. She would have known it. She was exactly like anybody else. Cleverer than her father?

"Not the test. What happened afterwards. You see, at that time they were planning a study of what they call gifted children."

"Gifted children? Gifted how? What's that supposed to mean?"

"In this case," her mother said, with heavy irony, " 'gifted' means 'very good indeed at doing IQ tests'. Well, they did a sort of talent-scouting affair round the schools, which was how you came to be tested. You were the age group they wanted, and your class teacher suspected that you were very bright. The idea was that the gifted children should attend a centre two afternoons a week for special teaching — harder work, to stretch them more — and their progress and development would be monitored very closely. It was an experiment, you see."

"But I didn't go."

"No. That's what troubled me. I wouldn't let you. And so of course I've wondered — was I robbing you of a chance, holding you back, depriving you of something — do you mind, Kim?"

"I don't mind at all. It sounds awful. Going off twice a week to a sort of clever-clever school — I don't like clever-clever kids anyway — and think how I'd have been teased!"

Mrs. Tate looked vastly relieved. "And from what I've seen of your reaction to educational psychologists, I don't think you'd have liked the idea of being watched, and studied,

155

and they'd have written no end of reports on you . . ."

"Ugh! No. Horrible. Is that why you didn't let me go?"

"Oh no. I hadn't even thought about that aspect of it. It was just a gut reaction. I didn't want you to be pushed in that direction — perhaps I was wrong, I don't know, but I just had this image of solemn humourless little kids with glasses sitting indoors poring over encyclopaedias — never having any fun — that was my picture of how they'd turn you out — and what's IQ anyway? I didn't want you to turn out like your father."

The bus lurched round a corner. Kim grasped the rail of the seat in front.

"What d'you mean? Dad's not humourless! He does have fun! How can you say that?"

"Oh, it's impossible to talk to you about your father."

"Why? And I'm not like him, anyway. I wish I could be. But I'm not. So it worked, didn't it?"

"You'd never have been like him. You've got his intelligence, yes, but my personality. You know you have. They could have mentally force-fed you for years and you'd not have been like him. I didn't know that then. I do now. You were born different. And why do you want to be like him anyway? You enjoy your life far more than he ever has. You're *better*."

"How can I be better? I don't care about IQ points. He is cleverer than me. Much."

"I said better, not cleverer! You know damn well what I meant. With him it's all in one direction. Abstract thought. He's never *done* anything with all this brain. Yes, I know he's writing a book *now*, but he's nearly forty! You're a much more balanced person. An all-rounder. It's healthier. It's what I hoped you'd be. That's why I've never cared much about your school marks. Look, Kim. Last term you came second in Maths, second in the high jump, second in the two hundred metres; you were in the school play, the

156

netball team, you joined the dance club. Well, your father would have been first in Maths, and he wouldn't even have *tried* any of the other things. That's the difference. And it's better to be you."

Yes, she'd been second in Maths, and second in three other subjects, and second in the form altogether, which must mean that either that test had been wrong or else Laura Willis was even more gifted than she was. Obviously. And then it occurred to her that she hadn't really worked all that hard for the exams — not hard at all — and it was well known that Laura swotted herself into a purple fug. So maybe it wasn't such a bad thing, if it meant she could get by in exams without over-exerting herself. It just wasn't very important; it didn't seem to mean anything. Certainly it was nothing to get so worked up about. Parents had some very odd ideas. From what her mother had said at first, Kim had expected the most horrendous disappointment.

"I wonder if Anna's gifted, too."

"Don't even think about it," said her mother. "I sometimes think I'm the only nice *average* person in the family. No, there's Frances. Thank God for Frances. So you're not mad at me, Kim? It was such a long time ago."

"No. I told you. I'm *grateful*." Clever-clever, as she called it, was not, by Kim's standards, at all an attractive thing to be. Nor did it fit in with her picture of herself.

"One day, you'll use your talents to good advantage. Till then, don't think about it. You're exactly the same as you were yesterday. Nothing's changed."

"*Every*thing's changing. Everybody's starting to do something new in September. Except me. Kerry's starting school. Anna's starting on Saturday Kidsline. Frances is starting at Thornton Park. You're starting a new job. I was wondering if there was still enough time left for anything to happen to me. Do you think this counts? Have I got to start being gifted?"

"God forbid," said her mother. "And of course you're starting something new in September. You're starting your training on the road to an Olympic gold at the high jump."

"Oh, yes!" said Kim. "That's it. I'll be a gifted high jumper. Come on, or we'll miss our stop."

12

"THERE WAS A CALL FOR you, Mum," Frances said. "Just a quarter of an hour ago. Mr. Truman. I said you'd ring back when you got in. I wrote the number on the pad."

"I don't suppose he's going to sack me, since I don't actually start work till Tuesday . . ."

"He didn't sound in a sacking mood," said Frances. "He sounded rather pleased. Is it all right if I go now?" She was spending the night at Janice's house.

"Yes, of course. Have a nice time. And would you know what a sacking mood sounds like? You should have heard dear Mr. Wilshire, just before he threw me out on to the streets. All loving kindness. It's called softening the blow. Let's be civilized about this, Mrs. Tate. Let's not make it any more unpleasant than we have to . . ." She went out into the hall, and dialled.

"Is he really going to sack her?" Anna asked with interest.

"Of course not," Kim and Kerry said simultaneously. The door banged behind Frances. Anna went over to the door and eavesdropped. "Yes. I'm sure she'll be very pleased," Mrs. Tate was saying. This sounded promising. Who would? "Thank you very much — yes, of course. Thank you for asking." Asking what? Unless she had positive proof to the contrary, Anna always assumed that every conversation she overheard was about herself. Perhaps they were going to ask her to make a personal appearance at the Thorn Centre, to sign autographs. "I'll see you on Tuesday, then. Have a nice Bank Holiday. No, nor are we. Good-bye." Anna beat a rapid retreat and sat, innocently, on the settee. In came her mother, beaming.

"Well, isn't that lovely? Fancy him asking . . . you know the Duke's coming to open the Centre? Well, the Duchess is coming too, and they want a smallish child to present her with a rather splendid bouquet. And Mr. Truman remembered my little moppet with the red hair, and he wondered if . . ."

"Kerry!" Anna leapt to her feet, eyes blazing. It couldn't *be*. "Why her? Why wouldn't he want the youngest? What's wrong with him? I'm much smaller than her! I . . ."

"Well, I'm sorry, Anna, but he's never seen you. *You* chose not to come to the Centre. You had to stay in in case the phone rang. It was your decision. You were invited. He's met Kerry. He remembered her. Naturally he asked her."

"But . . . " Oh! It was mean! Why hadn't her mother *told* him that she had another daughter who would be much better . . . The Duke *and* the Duchess . . . their son just two years older than herself . . . they'd probably bring him with them . . . she'd never have a chance like this again . . . she couldn't bear it! "Kerry!" She ran and threw her arms around her sister's neck. "Kerry, please let me do it instead of you. Please, please. I'll give you anything in the world. I'll let you have the bed by the window — anything — all you have to do is say to Mr. Thing that you don't want to do it and he won't mind a bit . . . Kerry I'll do anything for you but please let me give the Duchess the . . . "

"Shut up," said Kerry. Anna gasped. "All right. You'll give me anything?"

"Yes, anything!"

160

"Right. I'll have half your money."

"What money? I haven't got any money!" Kim and their mother watched, spellbound.

"The money they're going to pay you for doing Kidsline. Twenty pounds every fortnight. I'll have half of it."

"What?" Anna's face fell; she looked stunned. "But that's my wages! I'm a professional. You can't have that!"

Kerry shrugged. "It's up to you."

"But . . ." — oh, this was cruel! This was blackmail! "What would you want with money? What would you do with it?"

"Save it up," said Kerry, "until I've got enough money to buy an Old English sheepdog, and to feed it." Kim gave a gasp of admiration. It was brilliant. It was masterly.

Anna squirmed. It was cheating. It was diabolical. They should never have told Kerry she had distemper; see what it was doing to her? Her *money* — but the Duchess — she'd probably have her photograph in the *Thornton Gazette*: 'The bouquet was presented by local celebrity Anna Tate, beautiful blonde star of Kidsline' . . ."All *right*," she said through clenched teeth. "But you're a very greedy girl, Kerry Tate! You always want everything! You always get your own way!"

"And I'll have the bed by the window as well," Kerry said, receiving this onslaught with equanimity. Anna gave a tortured grunt and ran from the room. It was the end! It was too much! But the thought of the bouquet, and herself on the end of it, quickly soothed her. She couldn't work herself up to be properly angry with that to think of . . . to plan for . . . Soon she was rummaging through her wardrobe, trying to decide what she would wear. Nothing was good enough. She'd have to get on to Dad about that new dress after all. She thought perhaps a very pale blue. A girl could have too much pink in her life . . .

Downstairs, Kim and her mother had collapsed.

"Oh dear," Mrs. Tate said eventually, wiping her eyes. "Her face! Well done, Kerry. That was gorgeous — I'll have to ask Mr. Truman, of course. But I'm sure he won't mind."

"The only thing," said Kim, "you should have said *all* the money. She'd have had to agree. She couldn't have endured for you to have presented that bouquet. It would have killed her."

"Well, I didn't want to push my luck," Kerry said serenely. "Imagine if she'd said no. I'd have ended up with no dog money *and* I'd have had to present that bouquet."

"Don't you want to?"

"Of course not. I hate things like that. I was going to ask her if she'd do it anyway. But since she *said* she'd give me anything . . ." This set Kim off again.

"Well," Mrs. Tate said, "I'll see that she keeps her half of the bargain. What I'll do is to open a building society account for each of you, and the money can go straight in."

"Good," Kerry said. "Mrs. Hanrahan told me that if ever I got the money to have a dog she'd give me the address of the people that bred McCluskey. They're very good, you see. So I'll not only get a good dog, it'll probably be very closely related to McCluskey."

They had a lovely evening, the four of them. Everyone was in a good temper; each of them, in her own way, had good reason to look forward to the future. They had pizza; they watched television for a while, and then played 'What's My Line', which was a thing that only happened when everyone was feeling happy. They were still hard at it when the clock struck half past nine.

"Is it really that late? Where's the time gone? You two really must go up to bed."

"But we're in the middle of guessing what Kim is! We can't stop now!" Anna liked 'What's My Line'. She was very good at it.

"We'll just finish this one, then. It's still my turn, isn't it? Let me just recap, Kim. You travel around a lot in your work. You don't work with your hands. You provide a service."

"That's right."

"Are you quite sure it's nothing to do with death?" It was an understandable question. Already that evening Kim had been a grave-digger and a taxidermist.

"No. Definitely not."

"Right. That doesn't count as a no, you were agreeing with me . . ."

"Of course it's a no," said Anna. "Good. My turn. Now, you're doing a service, Kim. You're doing something useful."

"No. Not at all."

"But it's a service! It's got to be useful! You can't say no."

"She *did* say no," Kerry said. "It must be a useless service." Kerry, too, was a skilled and experienced questioner. "Is that right, Kim? You do something useless for people."

"Yes."

"This isn't possible," Mrs. Tate said. The taxidermist had been bad enough. And as for the plastic surgeon — 'I see a lot of blood in my work' . . .

"Do you go to people's houses to do it?" Kerry asked. "Is that why you travel around?"

"Yes."

"Do you have to touch people?"

"No."

"She's already said she doesn't use her hands," Mrs. Tate said. "Am I right in thinking you're not self-employed, Kim?" It had to be phrased that way, to avoid getting a no.

"Yes."

"You're not self-employed. Ah." It didn't help. "You work for a private firm?"

163

"Yes."

"So is this right — somebody rings your firm, and they send you round, and you do whatever it is that you do, and then you go back, and they send you out somewhere else."

"Absolutely right."

Mrs. Tate thought for a while. Anna wriggled; she didn't enjoy other people's turns, especially when they took so long about it.

"So I ring up, and you come to my house . . . "

"No."

"What?"

"Not to *your* house. I never said that."

"But . . ."

"You got a no!" said Anna. "It's *me*. Kim, you mean what happens is that people ring up and tell you to go somewhere else? I know! I know what you are. You're an inspector from the Cruelty to Children people. Someone reports that someone else is hitting their children and you go round to see."

Kim looked amused. "No. You couldn't be wronger."

"You couldn't call that a *useless* service, Anna," said her mother. "Come on, Kerry."

"Are you on your own when you go to all these houses?"

"Yes."

"Does whoever you do the service for have to be there when you do it?"

"Definitely yes."

"But the person you do it for isn't the person who asked you to do it?"

"That's right."

"Um." Kerry frowned. This was a horror. "Could *any-body* do this job?"

"No."

"My turn," said Mrs. Tate. "So we've established, Kim, that you're unqualified and useless. But not anybody can do

164

this job. Can it be done by either a man or a woman?"

"Yes."

"So do you, then, have some special ability?"

"Yes."

"Ah. There's something you can *do*. Can any of *us* do it?"

"No. Not well enough to do this job."

"You got a no," said Anna, rather crossly; she couldn't work this one out at all. "Is it an unusual job?"

"Very."

"Have I ever seen anybody doing it?"

"No—well, perhaps on television. but that doesn't…"

"Oh yes it does count. I'm going to *recap*." This was a way of stalling, when you couldn't think of a question. "You're going round all these houses, and none of the people you see have asked you to go, and you do the same thing at every house, and it's useless."

"And she doesn't use her hands, and there aren't many of her about, and she's got some particular ability."

"Does what you do take *long* to do?"

"No."

"Are the people you visit pleased to see you?" asked Kerry.

"Yes."

"Ah. You give them something."

"No."

"Oh help."

"Kim, do you have to go to houses?" Mrs. Tate asked. "I mean could you go and do what you do at an office, or . . . or . . ."

"I could do it absolutely anywhere," said Kim. "I could do it in the middle of the street. Standing on my head."

"Oh, this is ridiculous. We'll be here all night. One more question each, only. Kim, do you have to wear special clothing? Of any sort?"

"I wouldn't *have* to. But I should think I might. I *could*

165

do it stark naked . . ."

"You *could*," said her mother, "be arrested for causing a breach of the peace."

"Do you mean a uniform?" asked Anna.

"Yes, why not?"

Everyone looked glum. They hadn't considered the possibility of a uniform. It ought to help, but didn't. And only Kerry's question left. They looked at her, hopefully.

"If I saw you in your uniform," said Kerry, "would I recognize it and know what you were?"

"I doubt it," said Kim, who was enjoying herself very much.

"We'll have to think about it," said Mrs. Tate. "We'll try again tomorrow. Perhaps someone'll have a brainwave during the night." The Tates never, ever gave up. The only way to find out an answer was to guess it. One of Frances's more outlandish occupations had once been guessed seven months and eight days after she first thought of it; at any one time there would be at least two problems hanging around, waiting to be solved. During the Guessing Season (which ran roughly, from November to February) there might be as many as six. It was the one form of his puzzle mania which Mr. Tate had passed on to the rest of his family. He, of course, was much the best guesser. It wasn't nearly as good without him.

Anna and Kerry went reluctantly up to bed, still wrestling with the problem. Anna could not *bear* to be beaten. She would work it out in bed. Or perhaps Kim could be persuaded to give them a hint, when she came up to read to Kerry.

Kim gave no hints. She read a chapter of *Heidi*, and refused even to *discuss* 'What's My Line'. And as if that wasn't bad enough, Anna had returned from the bathroom, washed and well-daubed with Peachy Pink Talc (it smelled so nice) to find Kerry in firm occupation of the bed by the window, and herself mercilessly uprooted. She glared malevolently at the usurper. It was too bad. But — all the same — the Duchess — she must work on her speech — what did you call a Duchess anyway? Was she a Royal Highness? Oh — perhaps it wasn't such a bad bargain after all. Because even if Kerry got this dog, Anna would be its true owner. Kerry could look after it, but she would own it. It would have been paid for with *her* hard-earned cash. She would make this clear. Oh, and it didn't matter about the bed. She'd get it back, sooner or later.

Kim went back downstairs and made herself a glass of orange squash.

"Do you work regular hours?" Mrs. Tate asked hopefully. Kim gave her an enigmatic smile. "Oh well. It was worth trying. What are you going to do now? There's snooker on television, if you want to watch it."

Kim decided against it. She rather thought she'd go and have a bath. It was the last thing she thought before the phone call.

It all seemed so ordinary at first. Kim heard: "Oh, hello, Paul. How are you?" before her mother closed the door. Well, good. Her father would only today have received the letter telling him about Kerry's dyslexia — they *should* have let him know before — and, really, the surprising thing was that he hadn't rung earlier. He would probably want to come round and see Kerry; take her out, maybe. He hadn't been to the house once since he sold the car. It was so much more difficult for him without it. He didn't like walking at all.

Her mind wandered back to the 'What's My Line' game. Kim loved to be unguessable; it was a *civilized* way of getting the better of Anna. Anna's frustration was so strong as to be almost visible, an electric stormcloud hovering over her head, and sparking darkly from her ears and nostrils. It would be a long time before Anna thought of a singing

167

telegram. Or so Kim hoped. Particularly after the taxidermist, which had been guessed almost immediately. Kim had expected great things of the taxidermist.

And the minutes ticked away. Ten. Twelve. The house had gone very quiet. Thirteen. Kim got up and went over to the door. Silence. She opened it a crack. The hall was empty.

"Mum?" Kim walked, almost on tiptoes, to the foot of the stairs. Something was wrong . . . why was it so quiet? She didn't like it. She *wanted her mother*. "Mum!"

"I'm here." In the kitchen.

"Mum? What's happened?" Mrs. Tate was gazing out of the window. Her expression was indecipherable. "Is Dad all right?"

"Dad? Oh yes. He's fine."

"Then what is it? What's the matter? You weren't like this a minute ago. What did he say?"

Mrs. Tate turned round slowly, went to a stool and sat down.

"The book," she said, "is not two-thirds finished. Not by any means."

"Oh. Was he — exaggerating?" Oh, Dad. *Always letting me down* . . ."How much has he done?"

"He hasn't started it yet," her mother said tonelessly.

"What? But why would he tell you that? I *know* he's started it. Mum, I've *seen* it!"

"You haven't, you know. We've just been working out that you two had what must be the classic cross-purpose conversation of all time. Those pieces of paper aren't the book. They're just the preliminary background *notes*. Research. *That's* what he thinks he's done two-thirds of. He can't think how you came to misunderstand. Nor can I. Can't you tell the difference?"

"They didn't — I thought — it was all done in his speedwriting and I couldn't read it — I thought he was going to type it out nicely after he'd finished . . . oh, Mum, don't be

168

angry with me. I wish I hadn't said anything . . . I'm sorry," she said miserably. "I'm just sorry, that's all."

"Don't bother being sorry. You meant well, I suppose." Kim groaned. That was, in its way, quite as bad as being accused of deliberate spite. "It's worse for you, really," her mother went on. "You've been under this — illusion — all the time, haven't you? I've only had a few weeks of it."

"I'm sorry," Kim said again. She was apologizing for her father more than for herself. "You were so *happy*."

"I'll get over it. There was always a part of me that doubted. I know him so much better than you do."

"He said — he said, only six months to go and then the real fun would start . . ."

"That's right. Writing the book. What did you think he meant?"

"Having it published. But — oh, Mum, it's already more than a year and a half he's been gone . . ."

"Yes. And he hasn't started to write it yet. Quite possibly he never will. Why should he? He's having fun. Poking about in books all day — books about his precious Russia — pretending to call it *work* — he loves poking around in books." Echoes of Frances — echoes of David — "It'll be a different story when it comes to actually constructing a *book* from all these endless notes. That *is* hard work. I dare say he might start it. But he won't finish it. He's never yet finished anything in his entire life."

"Mum!" She didn't care if it was true or not; she didn't want to hear it. No; it was because she knew it *would* be true that she didn't want to hear . . .

"He hasn't. He didn't finish university. He could have got a first class honours degree standing on his head. But he dropped out in the second year because he was bored. He was writing a book when I met him. You didn't know about that, did you? He never finished it. He started a course that would have qualified him for a much better job. When I'd

169

just discovered I was expecting Anna. God, we needed the money. But he couldn't even finish that! Tell me one thing he's ever finished."

"He finishes the Mephisto Crossword," Kim said desperately. "Every week." It was all she could think of.

"The Mephisto Crossword! Well, Kim, there you have the measure of him. The Mephisto Crossword! And you wonder why I didn't want you growing up to be like him! He's wasted all his talents. Wasted. He's never done anything."

Kim couldn't speak. She wanted to cry out, but her throat had gone dead and numb. All of her was numb. She felt as if a huge part of her was being wiped out.

"And even if he does finish the book. Just suppose, for a moment, that he will. Why should he assume it would be a best seller? Any fool knows that you can't just decide to write a best seller, however much you study the trends. If it worked like that everybody would be doing it. By the time his book was finished and accepted and published the trends would be quite different anyway. It's obvious." Yes. It was. "And he's never set foot in Russia! How can he expect to convey any real *feeling* of Russia, when he's only read about it in books? It would be *phoney*. Other people's impressions. Nothing new or original. It's all just an academic exercise. Playing at being a writer. That's all it's ever been. I knew it from the start."

"Then why didn't you say! Why did you let him go!"

"Do you honestly imagine that anything I said would have made the slightest difference? Do you think I could have stopped him?"

"Oh, Mum. I thought — I thought it would all be over by Christmas . . . and what's he going to do when the car money runs out? How's he going to live?"

"Given up his job, has he? I thought so. Quite frankly, I don't care how he lives. *He* hasn't cared about *us* . . . He'll just have to do what everyone else does, and work. The cheek of it! Selling our car and living off the money . . . when I'm working full-time to keep us . . . I wish I'd never been such a fool as to let him *have* the car. We could have used it. We used to drive out to the country . . ."

"Mum," Kim said slowly. "He's never going to come back, is he?"

"No. I'm sorry, Kim. But the writing's been on the wall for long enough. I can't help it if you refused to read it. Everyone else knows. Even Anna knows. I'm sorry. I know you always loved him more than me. He'd be sitting in the armchair, smoking his pipe and teaching you to play chess, and I'd be running around doing a job and doing the house-work and the shopping and seeing that the bills were paid and bringing up four children on my own — yes, I do mean on my own — and naturally you loved him best. I'm sure a peaceful parent is much more pleasant than a harassed one. But there you are. Even if he wanted to come back, I wouldn't have him. Not now. I'm managing very nicely on my own. He wouldn't fit in here. He never did, really."

"Don't you love him any more?"

"Yes, actually, I do. In a way I expect I always will. But I still wouldn't have him back. Love wouldn't be enough, you see. You need respect, as well. He's not a bad man. He's never done a malicious thing in his life. But he should never have had a family. He's got no idea of responsibility. He's very much like a child. That's why I can never quite bring myself to resent him. He's so totally unaware that anything he does can affect anyone but himself. There's never any ill-will. If you tell him you're hurt, he's just rather puzzled . . . So I expect we'll be divorced, sooner or later. Or maybe not. It won't make much difference. Nothing's going to change. We'll be all right. Two things I'm going to say to you, Kim, and then I'm going to bed with a couple of sleeping tablets, and please don't call me in the morning.

Two things. One — don't ever marry somebody with whom you've nothing in common. However madly you may be in love with them. It's not enough. The love won't always be quite as mad, and there'll be nothing else to hold you together, when it's gone. And two. Don't ever be tempted to go on having children in the hope that it'll mend your marriage. Because, however much you adore the children, and however glad you are that you had them, it doesn't work."

Kim slumped. She knew that when she did cry, it would be very bad indeed, and it would go on for a long time, and when it was over she would feel better. Until that time the pain and the misery would possess her. She hoped she would cry soon.

13

THE HOT DOG MAN WATCHED as the girl with the Old English sheepdog came out of the park. They exchanged smiles; they were old friends. He often wondered about them. The girl wore a Thornton Park blazer; she was tall and slight — thirteen or fourteen, he reckoned. As for the dog, it was a handsome beast, still young — two years old, three at most. It had a strangely lethargic manner. She was a good girl, to walk it regularly. Not all kids bothered.

He leaned forward, suddenly. Were his eyes deceiving him? The girl had stopped — and she was writing on the wall! Well! He wouldn't have believed it. She nearly always stopped to read — but writing? A graffiti artist? She didn't look the type, somehow.

She finished, and moved away. The hot dog man stretched forward, peering, but his eyes weren't all they had been, and he couldn't make out the words. He couldn't bear it. He had to know. He climbed down from the van and crossed the road. Well, well. Now, just what did that mean? Underneath

DYSLEXIA RULES K.O.

the girl had written:

OH NO, IT DOESN'T!
KERRY TATE

And the coppery head disappeared round the corner.